Magic Force
The Beginning

By
Arrick Haun

PUBLISH AMERICA

PublishAmerica
Baltimore

ISBN: 1-60672-753-2
PUBLISHED BY PUBLISHAMERICA, LLLP
www.publishamerica.com
Baltimore

Printed in the United States of America

Magic Force
The Beginning

Prologue

Kimberly was a young twelve-year-old girl going onto thirteen. She had perfectly pure white skin, brown hair, and blue eyes. Today was her birthday. Her friend, Flower, came in the house. Flower was her childhood friend, she was younger than Kimberly by five months. She had blonde hair with white and slightly tanned skin with gentle blue eyes.

"Kimberly, your brother just arrived!" Flower said to her.

Kimberly was overjoyed at the sound of her brother's return. Recently her older brother Tommy had enrolled in the military. He was seven years older than she was. Kimberly ran into the hallway when she heard the door open. Tommy held up his hands and allowed his younger sister to run into his arms. He knew why, she supported him greatly and he was the only male in the family. Their father died when Kimberly was born. So he had to take the role not only as an older brother but also as a caring member of the family. He hugged Kimberly fondly pressing his hands around her soft brown hair.

"Kim I'm here, how has my younger sister been?" Tommy asked.

Kimberly lifted her head, not even bothering to open her eyes said "I've been doing fine"

"That's good"

Kimberly opened her eyes.

"Kimberly I have a surprise for you. Mother says you can keep them. Come on girl close your eyes and follow me to the basement." Kimberly looked confused and looked at Flower whom shrugged not even she knew the surprise. Kimberly finally closed her eyes.

"Flower you can come along. Come along young lady" Tommy ordered.

Flower obeyed and walked towards the door.

"Should I close my eyes too?" Flower asked.

"No, not at all, Kimberly has to because she is the new mistress of these gifts I'm about to give her. Just don't gasp when you see them young lady."

"Um, are you feeling okay Tommy? If so you can call me Flower. Oh Kimberly did you here all that you are the new owner of these gifts" Flower said.

"Yes" Kimberly said.

Indeed Kimberly heard every word of it. She couldn't open her eyes but she heard every word that passed between her brother and her friend.

Once Tommy, Flower, and Kimberly were in the basement, they stopped. Flower took a look around the room and saw a big huge gift and another one that looked like a horse.

"Now Kimberly you may open them," Tommy said.

Kimberly opened her eyes and gasped at the gifts.

"Happy birthday sis you may open them" Tommy said.

Kimberly's mother came down the stairs and placed her arm around her son's neck.

"Happy birthday Kimberly" she said.

"Happy birthday!" Flower shouted.

Kimberly opened the large gift first. Both Kimberly and Flower gasped at the huge height of the creature. It was a huge Battlebot. It had beautiful dark blue legs and arms. It had gold hands and feet, with an emerald green chest with ten sets of ruby red triangles going up and down joining in some kind of lock in the middle of the chest. Its head was black with a samurai mask over its eyes, which were the color gold. It wore a golden cape behind it.

Kimberly gasped, "It's huge!"

Flower took a ruler and measured the robot.

"It's about ten feet tall"

Kimberly looked at the huge robot for a while then opened the horse shaped one. She jumped out of the way as the present came to life. It was a unicorn about the size a real horse. It had white fur, a golden mane with a gold tail.

"You are lucky" Flower mumbled happily for her friend.

"These are for you Kimberly. Both the Battlebot and unicorn have served me well. They will also serve you well. Please take good care of them. They have been ordered to defend you" Tommy said.

"But don't you need guards?" Kimberly asked.

"No, hey you two please protect her and introduce yourselves" Tommy ordered.

The Battlebot saluted and spoke first "I am Goldsupervena. I live to serve and protect you"

"I am Moonshine. I am yours to command" the unicorn said.

"Thanks" Kimberly said.

Tommy got up and left "I got to go Kimberly I hope to see you again."

He cast a secret wink to Goldsupervena and Moonshine. The two creatures made a secret nod back. Both unicorn and Battlebot knew they were given to Kimberly to protect and defend her. The two girls went to bed unaware that Kimberly's newest guardians were watching them.

Chapter 1
Reality

Kimberly woke up the next morning thinking the gifts her brother gave her was just a dream. She quickly got a shower and dressed in her usual school uniform a beautiful light blue shirt and a white skirt. She looked at Flower whom was sleeping peacefully. Then she looked at her clock. It was six o' clock and school didn't start for at least two more hours.

Flower groaned and got up evidently Flower wasn't a morning person. She got up and looked at Kimberly.

"Are we late for school?"

"No, it's six am"

"**WHAT?!**" Flower shouted and she dashed into Kimberly's bathroom with her clothes in her backpack.

Kimberly ignored her friend's comment "It's okay, school doesn't start till eight thirty."

"Who cares?! I want to go to school and talk about what we always do in the library for one hour" Flower said as she stepped out dressed in the same uniform.

"Speaking of talking, was I dreaming that I got a Battlebot and a Unicorn?" Kimberly asked.

9

"Well why do you doubt it. It might be real" Flower said.

"Let's find out."

"Fine with me."

The two girls ran into the kitchen there they stopped and watched as Goldsupervena helped Kimberly's mother prepare breakfast.

"So the Battlebot is real," Flower said.

"Why would Tommy give me a Battlebot that served him?" Kimberly asked.

Kimberly and Flower backed up and they backed into Moonshine. It took the girls a few seconds before they realized it. With fright Kimberly and Flower jumped.

"Gee, remind me never to stand here" Moonshine said.

"She... She...She is real" Kimberly said fainting.

Moonshine looked at her new mistress concerned for her.

"Kimberly time for breakfast!" Kimberly's mother said.

Flower looked at Kimberly's mother "Kimberly just fainted when she slammed into Moonshine."

"Moonshine wake her up" Kimberly's mother said.

"Okay" Moonshine said shaking her head. The unicorn's horn glue and in her paw held a pale of fresh cool water. The unicorn quickly poured the bucket of water of Kimberly's face waking her up instantly.

"She's real. I got a real unicorn, but why?" Kimberly asked sitting up and letting Flower help her up.

"Time for breakfast" her mother said.

The three humans went into the kitchen. Goldsupervena stepped out of the kitchen. He looked at the unicorn's sudden emotion. Luckily Goldsupervena was programmed to know emotions so he knew what her emotion was but he didn't know what was bothering her "What is it Moonshine?"

"Goldsupervena I know you're a Battlebot so you wouldn't know what I'm feeling totally. I've seen many legends and many prophesies in my life. So do you think Kimberly is the one Tommy predicts? She's too peaceful" Moonshine said.

"Being a Battlebot I do know what peace is but only enjoy little parts of it. I'm not programmed to understand your wisdom sometimes but Tommy says she's the one."

"True"

"I believe whatever Tommy says. Only time will tell if she is. Only the Magicsaber of Light can tell."

"Okay, but I guess we can wait but she fainted at the sight of me but before she did she said words that make me so sad to hear I guess she didn't believe that we were real."

"Well...that can mean something the way your thinking and another way. But I don't think that she was not thinking that unicorns are not real. I think she was thinking that she couldn't believe that we were the gifts Moonshine. If so she most likely thought we were a dream, after all, who can afford a Battlebot and a Unicorn?"

"That's true, your type of Battlebot model is very expensive and your about one hundred million dollars. Plus unicorns are expensive too like about five thousand dollars," Moonshine said.

"So you get the picture?"

"Of course, now let's stop talking we might look suspicious to Kimberly when she comes out" Moonshine said.

"Definitely talking about this"

"I just hope Tommy is right" Moonshine mumbled.

Kimberly and Flower ran out of the kitchen. Goldsupervena and Moonshine stopped and watched the two girls.

"Bye Mom, I'll see you tonight" Kimberly said.

"Bye Kimberly have a good day at school!"

Kimberly and Flower ran out the door. Goldsupervena and Moonshine followed.

"Wait till the others at school see this" Kimberly said as she turned to see Goldsupervena and Moonshine running towards the school.

"True. They'd be scared stiff" Flower said as she ran right beside Kimberly.

The girls really wanted to get to school and fast. So they continued running.

"Boy for two long legs, those girls are awfully fast," Goldsupervena complained.

Moonshine whom was faster than Goldsupervena but still slower than the two girls shook her head.

"Not meaning to be rude to you Goldsupervena, I think she doesn't know that we're following her"

"Definitely, hey Kimberly wait up!

"You're a slowpoke Goldsupervena, she doesn't know that you Battlebots were built for attack and defense that means you are slow"

Goldsupervena winced as the unicorn's words sank in "Moonshine you are right, but please don't insult my kind, please."

"Okay I won't I understand your feelings. Hey remember when we first met?"

"Yes, we got into all kinds of arguments"

"Now look at us were getting along. It won't look good between our species" Moonshine said.

Both Battlebot and Moonshine burst out laughing.

"That's true. Battlebots and Unicorns getting along with each other. That'll be the day."

The two friends kept on running to the catch up with the two girls.

Chapter 2
The Clash

Kimberly and Flower made it to the forest. The forest was a shortcut to the school the two girls often took to get to school. They were tired of running and walked towards the school. Somehow something told them that they were in danger.

Lately a gang had been lurking in the woods. They captured and killed young girls and dumped their bodies into a stream. Flower trembled and took one step. Her foot caught a tree root and then they heard a loud crack as the root snapped! Kimberly froze and looked around Flower and herself. Suddenly a cry echoed through the forest.

"The gang members run!" Kimberly shouted as she saw the shadows move deeper into the forest.

The girls took a deep breath and ran. The gang members were everywhere. Everywhere the girls went a gang member was out. It was not long before the girls were surrounded.

"We're toast" Flower said.

"We sure are" Kimberly admitted sadly. She hated to lose her life in such a short time.

The gang's leader came up to them.

13

"Let's see one, two girls our lucky day now don't speak or we'll kill you on the spot."

Flower let out a whimper. Kimberly just put her head down. The gang picked them up and tossed them over their shoulders, walked towards a tree and tied them up to it.

"Help us" Kimberly prayed.

Luckily help was not far away. For Goldsupervena and Moonshine got to the destination!

"Oh great I knew they were fast, but I didn't expect this" Goldsupervena mumbled.

"Indeed but try looking for them" Moonshine said.

The Battlebot and unicorn looked around. Suddenly as if by sixth since or by magic, Moonshine and Goldsupervena sensed something, it was a sense that told them Kimberly was in danger. Quickly the two friends rushed to where the gang had the two terrified girls. One touched Kimberly's arm. She kicked him right in the nuts, but was rewarded with a knifepoint at her throat by the leader.

"One more attempt to kick or harm my companion and you're a dead girl" he said.

Moonshine's eye filled with hatred as the leader tied a rope to Kimberly's neck. Flower was already in the same situation as Kimberly was.

Moonshine's eyes clouded with blood red mist as she remembered how a gang slew her own parents. Now it was going to happen to two teen girls. The Battlebot, Goldsupervena didn't even stop to bother Moonshine. Moonshine and Goldsupervena both hated gangs. With a madden roar and with much rage the two friends hurled themselves into the melee. The two fought like mad beasts. Gang members were trampled to death by Goldsupervena's huge feet. The huge Battlebot didn't seem to care if they survived or not. Gripping a sword handle he enlighten the blade. It was a Magicsaber! Both girls looked at the Magicsaber's light blue blade and then to each other as they heard it's magical powers that unleashed and controlled the blade. They watched as Moonshine stabbed with her horn, kicked with her hind legs knocking gang members unconscious, and blasted them with a magical beam.

The leader thought fast as he watched Goldsupervena's Magicsaber run a gang member right through the chest. The gang leader gripped Kimberly firmly and pointed a gun at her head. He looked at Goldsupervena and smiled at the Battlebot.

"Pathetic, is this who your looking for?" he said. He pricked Kimberly with his knife in her neck. Kimberly screamed and watched as blood poured from her neck wound.

Goldsupervena stopped fighting and looked at his mistress's situation.

"What is it that you want with her?" Goldsupervena asked lifting his Magicsaber up.

"Oh nothing really it's just that she is another victim. Her friend is as well. Now I give you a choice, you leave me and let me kill her in peace or I'll kill her right now."

Goldsupervena looked at the gang leader. "Once more, go, or I'll shoot her" the leader placed his hand to the trigger of the gun near Kimberly's head.

Moonshine galloped into view.

"This goes for you too unicorn!"

Kimberly watched as he brought his hand down to her neck. Quickly, she bit the hand.

The leader screamed and punched her rudely against the tree.

"Kimberly its no use!" Flower shouted.

"Listen to your friend girl" the gang leader said as he turned her so her back was turned to him. Kimberly trembled as he placed his gun at her head.

"Help" she cried.

Goldsupervena knew he had to do it. He lifted his Magicsaber and shot a beam out of its blade. The gang leader didn't see it coming he kept his eyes on the struggling girl. The beam hit his hand destroying

15

the gun and cut his hand completely off.

"**ARRGH!**" the gang leader shouted.

Moonshine made her move the heroic unicorn leapt into the air and kicked the gang leader's head. With a sickening crack Moonshine had killed the gang leader.

The rest of the gang stopped as Goldsupervena and Moonshine stepped in front of Kimberly and Flower.

"Your leader is dead! Now if we see you messing with Kimberly or Flower we will destroy you just like the ones that we killed today, leave us!" Moonshine roared.

"Let me at them, they'll only live to kill another day" Goldsupervena said with rage and wielding his Magicsaber expertly.

Moonshine shook her head "Let's free these girls we are not murderers like those gang members"

Goldsupervena nodded "I suppose your right old girl" He said as the towering Battlebot untied the two girls.

Kimberly and Flower stood gasping at Goldsupervena's Magicsaber.

"Go, those gang members will be back and with a new leader" Moonshine said.

The two girls nodded and raced towards the school and into the library. Goldsupervena and Moonshine watched from a safe range. Both Goldsupervena and Moonshine didn't know of the disaster that was about to strike…

Chapter 3
Evil Strikes

Terror the Assassin Drone watched the military base. The huge spider-like human robot watched the American forces evilly. His second-in-command, Goldsupervena's brother, Railbuster watched him. The Americans were so slow and didn't know what was about to strike. Terror the Assassin plotted to destroy the American army and take over the world. He liked nothing better. It was him that told the general of the base their loyalty was to them. So for the past years Terror had served destroying terrorist organizations. Now the joke was on the American army. Terror secretly worked for one person: himself and his new empire, the Machine Assassin Empire.

"So Railbuster is it true that the American's found the Magicsaber of Darkness?"

"Yes milord" Railbuster said.

Railbuster was an evil Battlebot. He was all black and white. He hated his brother Goldsupervena because the Battlebot was the only thing that could ever defeat him.

"Railbuster I must have that terrifying blade" Terror said.

"Okay, I have other good news for us all. My brother is nowhere near this place" Railbuster said.

"Good and Moonshine?"

Railbuster roared, "That unicorn is gone as well!"

Terror smiled his empire was strictly going to win this battle. Without Moonshine, or Goldsupervena to help them out they were in trouble. The unicorn's magic and Goldsupervena's broad courage and strength could help the Americans succeed.

"What were they thinking Railbuster?"

"Oh nothing milord they didn't know that we were going to turn on them."

"Are the troops in position?"

"Yes, milord"

"Good. It is time, spring the trap!"

"It shall be done"

In minutes Terror's robotic troops fired upon the US troops. Several troops fell wounded or killed under the surprise attack. Kimberly's brother, Tommy immediately knew what was wrong and organized a counter attack. American tanks came into view. Terror and his fellow Assassin Drones flung themselves into the tanks gradually destroying them. Electric Drones electrocuted troops to death. Terror's deadliest drone the Nuclear Drones used their radiation on every single troop that fought against them. Tommy's men equally fought the enemy on at every turn. The enemy outnumbered them three to one. As soon as one soldier took two drones out ten more stood in their place.

Tommy took a long look behind the counter, drones were everywhere. He urgently knew what to do; it was time for Magic Force to be summoned. He wrote a note addressed to Kimberly and Goldsupervena.

Dear Kimberly, *the military base will be destroyed by the time you get here. Terror the Assassin is going to be Earth's newest conqueror. He is unstoppable and his drone followers are in higher numbers. You are the one Kimberly that can release the magic within and bring peace to this world. Release the force that is destined to rise. Note if Goldsupervena gets this letter, it's time my Battlebot companion. Help Kimberly. She is the one, I don't know how, I just can sense it, please protect her at all costs she is the only one to save the planet from Terror.*

Suddenly he heard drones approaching he gave the letter to a pigeon. The pigeon flew undetected. Tommy turned and saw Railbuster breaking the safe and retrieve the Magicsaber of Darkness.

"**No!**" Tommy shouted.

Railbuster turned his murderous gaze to Tommy "Yes, Tommy now evil has two blades!" he turned and opened another safe to retrieve the Magicsaber of Light. "**WHAT**? It's a fake!"

Terror burst into the room US soldiers cringed at the sight of him.

"Railbuster what's going on?"

"Milord, the Magicsaber of Light it's gone!"

"What do you mean? Surely you got two handles!" Terror said shocked.

"No this ones a fake, watch a normal handle doesn't break like this" Railbuster snaps the handle into pieces! "In fact milord the only way to destroy a handle is by striking it with a Magicsaber blade, or the second way with brute strength mixed with very powerful magic."

Terror turned his own murderous glaze on Tommy.

"What?" Tommy asked.

"This is your doing human! Where is the Magicsaber of Light?" Terror asked his voice dangerously low.

Tommy gripped a flamethrower

"I won't tell where it is. Once your brother Goldsupervena, Railbuster finds out about this he will fight you," Tommy said.

Railbuster tossed Terror the Magicsaber of Darkness.

"You have one chance human. Now tell Terror where it is."

"Never!" Tommy pressed the gun trigger. The gun sent out a beam of fire at Terror. Terror was struck. The smell of burning armor filled the air.

Tommy stopped, as he thought, Terror wasn't a strong leader then he turned his eyes to Railbuster and lifted his flamethrower at the Battlebot. Railbuster smiled and a deadly hiss filled the air as Railbuster's red Magicsaber filled the area. Tommy fired the gun. Railbuster lifted his Magicsaber and reflected the blast back at Tommy. Tommy dodged the reflected beam but that cost him dearly. He slammed into Terror. He looked at Terror. The Assassin Drone stood there smiling then he enlightened the awful Magicsaber of Darkness and stabbed at Tommy. Tommy felt his life draining away as a deadly black blade concerning the powers of Darkness slowly claimed his life. Many troops that had survived didn't know where the Magicsaber of Light was so Terror didn't kill them. Terror watched as he kept them captives.

"By noon today you will all tell me where the Magicsaber of Light went" Terror said to them.

One soldier whispered to another "We're finished Terror has his grip on the Magicsaber of Darkness. The evil blade will slowly allow him to conquer the Earth. I just hope that Captain Tommy knew what he was doing. Plus I don't even know where that Magicsaber of Light went."

"Quiet! You'll get us both killed" another said.

The soldiers were led to a prison cell and thrown in and they were supervised by a twenty-four seven-hour guard.

Chapter 4
The Hero of Light

School was almost out. Kimberly told the principal of her Catholic School about the gang assault on herself and her friend Flower. The principal overwhelmingly agreed to put more police officers near the forest. Kimberly had told some of the other girls in her classes that she had a Battlebot and unicorn. Most boys and girls didn't believe her at first, but once they saw Goldsupervena and Moonshine come in they stopped and stared at them. Moonshine blushed as people started to pet her.

"Nothing like it Goldsupervena"

Most boys in Kimberly's school enjoyed the huge Battlebot and began to polish his armor.

"This is the life" the Battlebot sighed watching as his fist glowed with even more gold. Soon the Battlebot was sparkling all over. Suddenly both Goldsupervena and Moonshine stumbled forward. Kids scattered away not wanting to be poked by the Unicorn's horn or stepped on by a Battlebot's foot.

"Go to class people!" an Assistant Principal told them.

Kimberly for once looked at Goldsupervena and Moonshine.

Did I do something wrong? She thought.

Goldsupervena looked at the assistant principal.

"If I can, madam I'd like to speak to my mistress"

The assistant Principal nodded and allowed Kimberly and Flower to talk to Goldsupervena and Moonshine.

"Did I do something wrong?" Kimberly asked them.

Goldsupervena shook his head "No, Kimberly my mistress, Moonshine and I can feel deaths"

Moonshine nodded "True. My magical powers are dangerous but they can also sense death. Kimberly, someone we all know has died."

Flower and Kimberly looked shocked "N.N.N.No Tommy's been killed!" Kimberly guessed.

"I believe so Kimberly"

"Who killed him?"

"That my sensors and Moonshine's magical powers can't tell. However I do remember one specific Assassin Drone" Goldsupervena said.

"**TERROR!**" Moonshine growled.

"I knew that spider was up to no good! I told them that but did the generals, commanders, and all but one captain listen to my feelings...**Nooo**" Goldsupervena said.

"Terror?" Flower asked.

"Who's Terror?" Kimberly asked.

It was Moonshine that growled the answer "Terror is an Assassin Drone. He claimed that he was going to help our American army if we took him in and protected his forces. He called his forces the Machine Assassin army! The military took him in and allowed him to help us. Goldsupervena here knew something was not right with that drone. So did I but not at that moment. Now I think that because we were gone Terror decided to attack the US Army!"

Kimberly looked outside "We'll know soon here comes my brother's pigeon."

The pigeon landed and gave Goldsupervena the letter. The

Battlebot read the letter and then sighed and secretly nodded to Moonshine.

"Kimberly this note's for you."

Kimberly took the note and read the letter.

"So... I-I-I-it's true" She wept, and ran out of the school.

The assistant Principal looked at Flower whom shrugged.

Moonshine took the advantage of the situation. "Apparently madam, Kimberly isn't skipping school. She just needs time."

The principal nodded and wrote down an early dismissal form for both Flower and Kimberly. Moonshine quickly signed the dismissal forms and along with Flower and Goldsupervena ran outside to where Kimberly was running.

A young man about same age of Kimberly saw her come out of the school. The boy could tell Kimberly was deeply saddened. The man's name was Kent Savior. Kent watched as a Battlebot, blonde haired girl, and a unicorn came out. The three creatures followed the girl that just came out. Kent immediately knew something was up. He leapt up onto his horse; Swift's back and raced through the countryside. He found Kimberly near the river's edge. The girl was weeping.

"Tommy... why now?" she asked herself.

Kent took a good look at the girl. Then realized that the girl was in his gym class. He touched her arm making her jump.

"Easy are you okay?" he asked her.

"Um, I was sad, but now I'm scared please don't hurt me" Kimberly said backing away.

"It's okay, I'm not here to hurt you. My names Kent what's yours?" Kent asked.

"Kimberly" Kimberly said.

Kimberly looked at Kent the boy meant every word he had said. He didn't want to harm her he just wanted to know what was making he so sad.

"So what's in the letter?" Kent asked.

"Oh, my brother, Tommy is dead. He is the only male in my family that I looked up to"

"Hmm. No wonder you're sad" Kent said.

"Um, yes. You feel my pain?" Kimberly asked.

"Sure would you like to take a walk with me?" Kent asked smiling at Kimberly.

"Um...Sure" Kimberly said looking at Kent.

Kimberly felt her heart melt within her. Was this what it felt to fall in love?

Careful Kimberly don't go that far she thought. But she disobeyed her own thoughts and took a slow walk with Kent.

Goldsupervena, Flower, and Moonshine stepped into the area. There they saw Kimberly with a young man.

"What was in the letter that upset her?" Flower asked Goldsupervena.

"Something wrong...you wouldn't want to know" Goldsupervena said.

"Kimberly don't fall in love with that boy!" Flower shouted.

"She can't hear you" Moonshine said.

"Oh..." Flower mumbled. "Goldsupervena charge him!"

Goldsupervena almost thought about charging unfortunately for him, Battlebots were not programmed to know one emotion...Love. He made an attempt to but Moonshine stopped him.

"So what if she found a boyfriend. I know Battlebots aren't programmed to know what love is but she's in love. She needs someone to talk to her. Humans need to talk to one another," Moonshine said.

Flower understood Moonshine's advice and nodded "I'll go to cheer her up" she said.

Once they were alone, Goldsupervena and Moonshine turned to each other.

"It's true that Tommy is dead right?" Moonshine asked.

"Yes, the base has fallen to Terror the Assassin" the Battlebot said.

Moonshine shook her head "They should've trusted your feelings and now America is going to be conquered."

"Hope isn't lost, fortunately before Tommy was killed, my sensors tell me that he died without telling Terror where the Magicsaber of Light was"

"So…It was because of the discovery of the Magicsabers of Light and Darkness that Terror turned against us. He wanted those blades so he can rule against us and there will be no one to oppose him!" Moonshine said kicking a stone up in the air and headbutting it with her anger.

"Yes, Tommy made a great move for the Americans, by programming me to protect the Magicsaber of Light that blade will never fall however it's evil twin has"

"Who has it? Your evil brother Railbuster?"

The mention of his evil brother stunned the Battlebot in his tracks.

"Sorry Goldsupervena" the unicorn said.

"Don't mention it, and for once my brother isn't the person of that Magicsaber. It is Terror that has his grip on the evil blade" Goldsupervena said sadly.

"Well…is it time?" Moonshine asked.

"Yes, the letter addressed me to give the blade to her"

"Then let's hope she is the one"

"Yes, let's or our research is gone"

The two friends walked down the path.

Kimberly and Kent looked into each other's eyes.

"Kimberly so, your sad because your brother is gone. That's really tragic" Kent said to her.

Kimberly looked down at the ground "Yes, I know. Now I'm the only one besides my mother in my family living."

Flower rushed down "Kimberly, I'm sorry that your brother is gone. But you've got to buckle up. I'm willing to bring his killer to justice."

"Really?"

"Yes"

Kent looked into Kimberly's eyes "Kimberly I'm willing too" "Good, but one problem who's his killer? And what does it mean when my brother said I was magical?" Kimberly asked.

"Good questions, but I don't think we have a good answer to those questions were all humans" Kent said.

"True, hey, Kimberly, Goldsupervena and Moonshine will hopefully know!" Flower said.

Goldsupervena and Moonshine both knew they were caught.

"Indeed we know what he means," Goldsupervena said.

Kimberly jumped and landed in Kent's opened arms "Goldsupervena, Moonshine, I didn't see you there!"

Goldsupervena nodded "Kimberly, listen remember when your brother gave you us. He told you that in time you will know why he gave us to you."

"Yes, I remember. I kept asking myself why" Kimberly said.

Moonshine nodded "He gave us to you because you are a likely contestant to wield the famous Magicsaber of Light."

Flower and Kent gasped "The Magicsaber of Light!"

Kimberly looked at Moonshine and Goldsupervena confused "What is the Magicsaber of Light?"

Flower looked at Kimberly in shock.

"Don't you know anything about the two special Magicsabers?" she asked.

"No, Tommy never told me about them"

"And for a good reason" Moonshine said.

Goldsupervena explained the two Magicsabers "The Magicsaber of Light is the strongest Magicsaber of all for the forces of good. It is capable of killing evil in one direct blow. All Magicsabers can fire beams out of their blades, but this part from the Magicsaber of Light can't kill in one blow it only kills in one blow in close combat."

Kimberly looked at her friends before looking at the Battlebot and unicorn "And Tommy believes I can wield that blade impossible!"

"Let's find out," Flower said getting excited.

Goldsupervena nodded he pressed his combination lock and reached in his chest and pulled a Magicsaber's handle out and he gave it to Kimberly.

"Please Kimberly. Please be the one," the Battlebot begged.

Kimberly nodded, grabbed the light gray handle and then pressed the ignition switch. The area around Kimberly began filling in with white shiny metallic light and then the handle released the Magicsaber's blade. Unlike Goldsupervena's blue Magicsaber the Magicsaber of Light was a white blade. Once the glow stopped Kimberly looked dramatically different. She looked no longer a schoolgirl in uniform but she looked like a leader. She wore a black tank top, black boots and an black skirt.

"I.I.I" Moonshine stammered.

Goldsupervena was also speechless but only for a minute.

"The Magicsaber of Light! It responds to Kimberly's touch only!" he shouted.

"I-I-I" Moonshine stammered.

Kimberly turned her gaze to the unicorn "Are you okay?"

The unicorn shook her head "I'm okay, Kimberly, just s-s-s-shocked, you see I doubted you Kimberly. I had my doubts but Goldsupervena is an expert in prophecy. He stays with them even though they might be fake until the last possible theory fails. Another thing is that I didn't expect to meet the wielder of the Magicsaber of Light."

"Oh" Kimberly said leaping out of Kent's hands and onto the ground below.

Kimberly gave it to Flower who touched the handle and upon doing so shut off the Magicsaber of Light.

"It is perfect. The Magicsaber shuts off as soon as someone not the person it chooses touches it" Moonshine gasped.

Kimberly touched the handle and the Magicsaber responded.

"Oh, Kimberly! You're the owner of the Magicsaber of Light" Kent said hugging her.

Kimberly for the first time didn't bother to stop him.

"Kent. I love you," she mumbled.

"Your cute too, Kimberly, want to be my…" Kent began.

"Girlfriend, sure" Kimberly said as he kissed her.

Flower gasped "Kimberly what will your mother think?"

Kimberly looked at Goldsupervena and then to Moonshine. Goldsupervena looked puzzled but Moonshine understood her mistress's look.

"Your secret is safe with me," the unicorn said.

"What secret?" Goldsupervena asked.

"She's in love," Moonshine said.

"Oh" Goldsupervena said, puzzled.

"Well, it's safe with me too" Flower said.

"Thanks, but Kent if my mom sees me like this she'll ground me for a week" Kimberly said.

"Once she finds out I'll explain everything so she'll understand it so you won't be grounded" Moonshine said.

"Thanks Moonshine, and thanks Goldsupervena for the Magicsaber of Light!"

This the mention of the Magicsaber of Light brought the Battlebot out of his trance "What the? Oh your welcome."

The five friends started on to walk home.

Chapter 5
Evil's Major Discovery

Terror looked around thousands of marines lay around him. His prisoners sat underneath in the prison cell. Terror looked at his slain victim Tommy. *Foolish man* the Assassin thought if you would've told me where the Magicsaber of Light was you wouldn't be dead. Railbuster stepped in.

"Ah…Railbuster I trust that you found out where the Magicsaber of Light is" Terror said.

"Actually, I haven't but I believe my brother has the Magicsaber of Light!" Railbuster said.

"What makes you think that, he is it's wielder!" Terror said.

A marine known as Sergeant Bash was brought in before Terror by his guards.

"Well why wouldn't my brother be here. Evidently, Tommy knew we would've had both blades in hand. That unicorn also knew about this so together those three hatched a plan. Now I remember Tommy talking about his sister" Railbuster said.

"Tell us more," a guard said.

Terror knocked the guard unconscious "Fool let him talk to me! Go on Railbuster!"

Railbuster bowed "The girl's name is Kimberly. She as her brother put it is strong and is the one to wield the goodly blade."

"Then she must die" Terror said.

"No!" Bash shouted. Terror looked at the marine "She's not your sister now. So why are you protecting her?"

"You Assassin, you killed her only brother and now you want to kill her. She's peaceful...oops," Bash shouted.

"Peaceful is she? Then Railbuster, I guess we can spare her life once. Ask her to give you the Magicsaber of Light. Steal it from her and bring it to me. With both blades the Earth is doomed!" Terror ordered.

"It shall be done Milord, taking the Magicsaber of Light from her should be an easy task. However my brother and that unicorn will be with her I can feel it now" Railbuster said.

"Then be extra cautious Railbuster, make your move carefully. Your brother will not let you convince Kimberly to give you the blade."

"Yes. But if she doesn't give me the blade?" Railbuster asked.

"Kill her then and take it!" Terror said.

"But Kimberly's only thirteen!" Bash shouted.

"Take him away we have no need for a thirteen year old girls except for one thing **SLAVERY!**" Terror said.

"Kimberly may be peaceful, but I'm pretty sure she will know what is right and wrong!" Bash shouted as he was dragged away. Terror looked outside his huge city he enlightened the Magicsaber of Darkness. He looked at evil blade and grinned. The evil blade glittered it's deadly light.

Chapter 6
The Encounter

Kimberly walked along the pathway. Her trusty companions, Flower, Kent, Goldsupervena and Moonshine walked behind her. Goldsupervena's senses something. Moonshine looked into the dark night her powers warned her evil was near. Then Kimberly stopped and saw a black robot similar to Goldsupervena. She saw the black Battlebot's red Magicsaber blade.

"Are you the one known as Kimberly Salah the owner of the Magicsaber of Light?" the Battlebot asked.

"Yes" Kimberly said.

"I demand that you give me that Magicsaber or else" the robot shouted.

"Or else what?" Kimberly asked.

"I will have no choice but to kill you" Railbuster said.

"Careful Kimberly this is my evil Brother Railbuster second-in-command of Terror's forces!" Goldsupervena said.

Kimberly looked at the glowing red blade.

"Never you slime! Your leader killed my brother! Why should I give you a blade for world domination?" Kimberly asked.

Railbuster smiled evilly "If you won't surrender the blade peacefully then I can kill you as well. If you surrender peacefully then I won't kill you."

The robot launched himself at Kimberly, his Magicsaber ready to spear her through. Kimberly jumped over Railbuster. He turned and to his surprise, his brother was in front of Kimberly.

Railbuster looked at Goldsupervena "We meet again my dear brother."

Goldsupervena's eyes filled with anger but his feelings were clear "You've lost that privilege of calling me your brother years ago!"

Railbuster jumped over Goldsupervena while Goldsupervena turned to one side and stomped Railbuster down on the ground.

"Still no match to me brother. You still try the same move every time. There is no way you can beat me with that move"

"So, how about this!" Railbuster lifted his leg off of him making Goldsupervena flip backwards onto his back. Goldsupervena barley blocked an attack by Railbuster. He stood up and started blocking attacks.

Throughout the duel Goldsupervena thought about the events in the past when his brother was on his side and not Terror's side. He thought of the battles he and his brother fought side by side. Those were the days for the two Battlebots. Then one day he learned the horrible truth. Railbuster was working along side with Terror. He remembered the duel before this one. Only the clash of the Magicsaber's brought him out of his thoughts.

"Brought you back to reality brother" Railbuster said.

"Are you ready to get your throat cut off?" Kimberly asked putting the Magicsaber of Light across Railbuster's neck. Goldsupervena stopped his attack.

"Railbuster, you were a really good brother but now I see that we are now enemies! You fight alongside Terror the Assassin now. I fight alongside the humans now. This is Earth and I'm not going to let evil win! I'm truly the Battlebot for the good side!" Goldsupervena shouted.

"Then so be it Goldsupervena my dear brother"
Railbuster pulled Kimberly off him and threw her off him.

"Kimberly, don't go back in there! It's too dangerous." Flower yelled

"Let her do so, Goldsupervena is superior in this type of fight in fact he's the best Magicsaber Fighting Battlebot meaning he's stronger than all of the other models of the Battlebots combined! He can teach Kimberly" Moonshine said.

"Then what can I do?" Flower asked.

Kimberly brought out the Magicsaber of Light and lighted it. The Magicsaber's white blade came out. It sent two beams. One beam was sent at Flower and the other one Kent. Kent leapt upon Swift's back but the horse was hit and turned into and warhorse. Flower looked shocked as the beam gave her and gave her a rifle. This rifle had a sniping tool and a big gun nozzle.

"The Magicsaber of Light has the powerful army that no one evil can withstand. It just gave you a Magic Sniping Riffle it turned you into a Magic Trooper and Kent into a Magic Caviler unit. Magic Cavilers can use Magicsabers of their own but are experts wielding them on horseback. However they can also wield other Magical items. Items such as Magic Lances, and Magic Axes" Moonshine explained.

"Cool, I feel like a Medieval Knight" Kent shouted.

"You look like one to, oh and looks like your in the uniform of a knight" Flower said.

Kent looked down and saw his armor. He looked at Flower "Your in armor too Flower. Problem is the armor is white. It is too bright a color it won't help us much as we stick out too much."

"We need a diversion," Flower said.

"Think of one now" Moonshine said.

"Why?" Kent and Flower asked.

"Kimberly just left" Moonshines said.

They watched Kimberly walk towards the Magicsaber dueling Battlebots.

Railbuster watched Kimberly come near the Magicsaber of Light in her hands.

"So you are the person to wield the Magicsaber of Light. Well I had my own doubts but now I have to kill you girl. Give the blade to me and I'll spare you" Railbuster said.

"Never Railbuster!" Kimberly shouted and she swung the Magicsaber of Light at Railbuster.

"You remind me of someone let's see who do you remind me of" Railbuster said catching Kimberly's blade easily in his own red blade.

Kimberly watched and parried another Magicsaber thrust from the evil robot.

"Oh, yes that is how your brother looked before he died" Railbuster sneered.

Kimberly sadden gasped and looked down.

"Yes, girl your thoughts about your brother betray you. You loved him dearly."

"Don't listen to him Kimberly" Goldsupervena said.

"Why don't you shut your mouth before I shut it for you" Railbuster shouted.

"Try to" Goldsupervena said as he parried his brother's blade.

"I'd be glad to" Railbuster said as he attacked Kimberly and Goldsupervena.

Goldsupervena was still superior and was greater than Railbuster. Kimberly was not so lucky, but learning how to wield the blade. The duel continued for thirty minutes. The red, and blue Magicsaber plus the white Magicsaber of Light clashed violently against each other.

"This is more like it" Railbuster said as he kicked Kimberly onto the path, onto the ground and on her Magicsaber. Luckily the powerful blade didn't spear her through.

"What???" Flower gasped as she saw the Magicsaber's blade not spearing Kimberly through the stomach.

"The Magicsaber of Light doesn't kill good people. It judges whoever lands on it. If it judges you pure evil or mostly evil it…well you know what it does instant death. If it judges you pure good, it'll just bounce off like a normal play sword" Moonshine explained.

"Oh watch out!" Flower shouted.

Railbuster raised his Magicsaber for the fatal blow "You've fought gallantly and now it's time to die!"

He struck out it was aimed at her head. Kimberly closed her eyes and waited for the moment of death. Suddenly a clash sounded and she opened her eyes, Goldsupervena's Magicsaber had caught the red Magicsaber.

"You'll regret defending Kimberly" Railbuster said.

"Then so be it" Goldsupervena told him.

The three resumed the position and attacked.

Kent leapt upon, Swift's back.

"I'm going to help them!" He shouted.

Flower lifted her Magic Sniper Rifle to her eye and looked through the sniping tool. Once she located Railbuster she fired the gun.

TWEEWWW!!! The gun fired a white-pinkish beam at Railbuster. Railbuster watched the blast come near him and with one swift strike parried Kimberly's Magicsaber of Light and Goldsupervena's Magicsaber plus reflected Flower's beam right back at her. Flower screamed once and with surprise fell and broke her legs and twisted her arm.

Kimberly watched as Moonshine raced towards her wounded friend and with her magical powers disrupted Railbuster's Magicsaber blast. Kent lighted his Magiclance and stabbed at Railbuster. He succeeded in making a hole in Railbuster's chest.

"ARRGH!" Railbuster cried looking at the hole in his chest. He attempted to slice Kent's head off but Swift was quick and got his master out of danger quickly.

Railbuster didn't have time to retaliate quickly for Goldsupervena sliced his right hand off.

"ARRGH!" Railbuster cried in pain as Goldsupervena's blade hit.

Railbuster stumbled Kimberly knew he was too far away for her to strike so she sent a blast from the Magicsaber of Light's blade. The blade's beam hit Railbuster in his opened chest wound. Railbuster fell and lifted his left hand up in a sign of defeat.

"Very well…you all have defeated me"

Kimberly raised her Magicsaber of Light to strike Railbuster down.

"Go on strike me down girl. Strike me down before I can get up. I am unarmed now," Railbuster said.

Kimberly looked like she was about to but sighed as Goldsupervena placed his hand on her shoulder.

"Don't do it Kimberly!" Moonshine warned.

"What can I do he'll just live to fight another day!" Kimberly shouted.

"True but if you kill him the negative thoughts that are in you will become part of the Magicsaber of Light's power. If you kill him with it the next time you land on it, it will remember what you've done" Goldsupervena said.

Kimberly looked at Railbuster

Railbuster sneered at her "Go on, avenge your brother's death."

Kimberly knew she was at a ransom and quickly came up with the decision.

"No, I can't kill you in cold blood" she said as she tossed her Magicsaber of Light down.

Railbuster waited for it to touch the ground but as if his senses told him, Goldsupervena caught the blade's handle and the blade turned off.

"Thank you Kimberly, you'll regret that you've spared my life. Once Terror finds out that you've defeated me he will send his armies out to fight you! You will fall, and burn into ashes and the Magicsaber of Light will be in our hands at the end," Railbuster said as he vanished in a cloud of smoke.

Kimberly bent down to her friend Flower "I couldn't kill him" she said.

"We almost had him too," Flower said.

"True but what he said was horrible did he speak the truth?" Kimberly asked.

Moonshine nodded "Battlebots are incapable of lying to anyone." Kimberly turned on her Magicsaber. The Magicsaber of Light turned on and sent out more beams. Out of the beams came an army of Magic Troopers and other Magic Cavalier units.

The Magic Troopers looked like Flower but wore a helmet and had white armor. Magic Troopers had oxygen tanks located on their backs and had their Magic Snipping Rifles. Kent ran to greet the other Magic Caviler units.

"You've got the beginnings of an army," Goldsupervena said.

Kimberly nodded as she raised her arm into the air "Let's go home, I want to talk to my mother about this attack on me and my brother! LONG LIVE MAAAGGGICCC FFFOOORRRCCCEEE!"

"Okay we'll obey then Lady Kimberly of Magic Force!" Goldsupervena shouted bowing to her.

Kimberly stopped and lowered her arm "Um, excuse me Lady Kimberly?"

Moonshine nodded and bowed to her "The Magicsaber is yours and you're the leader of Magic Force. You'll have to get used to it. Battlebots are programmed by the people that create them to speak professionally."

"Oh so, Goldsupervena will call me Lady Kimberly for now on?" Kimberly asked.

"Yes, Lady Kimberly I will" Goldsupervena said.

"Let's go home," Kimberly said.

It was five o'clock when they reached home. Even though Flower didn't know she broke her legs she weakly followed Kimberly, Moonshine gripped Flower and had her ride the rest of the walk it is then when she realized Flower's strength. She hated to tell Kimberly that the reflected blast of the Magic Rifle blast was a serious wound to Flower.

Kimberly got home holding Kent's hand. Kimberly's mother came out and saw Kent.

"Well, Kimberly what have I told you about being with boys" she scolded her daughter.

Moonshine stepped between the young girl and her mother.

"Listen, madame Kimberly is close to an adult don't you think it's time for her to have a relationship with a boy?"

Kimberly's mother was easily baited by the Unicorn's wisdom. "Yes, but…"

"Then it's time to let her have a boyfriend. Besides I've watched him myself, he's sweet to her and she is sweet to him back. See this wisdom?" Moonshine asked.

"Yes, I do, I guess I didn't see her grow up" Kimberly's mother confessed.

Then she looked at Kimberly "I guess you grown Kimberly. Just be careful with men. Oh and Mister, please take good care of her."

"I'm Kent maim, I will take good care of her" Kent said.

"Good. Oh my gosh Flower are you okay?" Kimberly's mother asked Flower.

"I'm fine" Flower mumbled as she jumped down as soon as she hit the ground she fell face first. She tried to take a step but as soon as she did she felt pain in her legs.

Kimberly's mother was a doctor and raced towards the struggling Flower. Then she noticed thousands of Magic Trooper and Magic Cavilers.

"So it's true Kimberly. You are the one that can wield the Magicsaber of Light! That's great now you can save the world from Terror"

"Yes, I guess you heard."

"I did, now Flower what happened to you dear?"

"Um, Goldsupervena's brother Railbuster reflected my Magic Snipping Rifle's blast and it hit me."

"You fell" Moonshine said.

Kimberly's mother scooped up the wounded girl and placed her on a step.

"Railbuster…So who was he after this time? You Flower?"

"No, mother" Kimberly said.

Kimberly's mother looked at her daughter "Then who?"

"It wasn't who, it was a thing and that thing happened to be my Magicsaber of Light" Kimberly said.

"Now that she's fought against him, he and Terror will be back to kill the ones that harmed him" Goldsupervena said.

Kimberly looked down "Me first, then you Goldsupervena, then you Kent."

Kent placed his arm around her neck.

"It's okay. With an army of this size we could protect ourselves. You and me are easy targets but Goldsupervena's a tough target, I'd like to see them try to destroy him."

Kimberly looked at Goldsupervena with admiration "True he could take a lot down before they could harm him."

Kimberly's mother looked around and held Flower's two legs "Kimberly, don't agree to go out and engage Terror he's too dangerous."

"She doesn't have to but Terror will succeed in invading this country if Magic Force doesn't do something" Flower said.

"Right out of my mind" Moonshine said.

"And what's scary for you humans is to realize it, she's right" Goldsupervena said.

"That's also true" Moonshine said.

"Mom, someone has to take a stand, I don't want the USA to fall to an invincible enemy! That someone is me, no matter the cause, Goldsupervena, Moonshine are you with me?" Kimberly asked.

"I'm ready to serve you Lady Kimberly" Goldsupervena said bowing down to his leader.

The unicorn bowed to Kimberly "I'm also ready, our lives are in your hands Kimberly."

"Thanks" Kimberly said.

"Kimberly I'm coming with you. I am with you till the end" Kent said.

"Gee, you are a nice young man" Kimberly's mother said moving Flower's leg.

"OW!"

"Oh dear sorry, Flower."

"I'm coming too Kimberly" Flower told her.

"Gee, thanks my friends but, um, are you okay?" Kimberly asked.

"Ow, yes, oh I mean no!" Flower said.

"True her legs are broken" Kimberly's mother said as she ran into the house and got two leg casts.

She wrapped Flower's legs in the casts "Since you have you both legs hurt, you'd have to ride something for a long time for your legs to get better and that bullet wound in you chest is bleeding."

Kent picked Flower up and looked to both Kimberly and her mother "Swift can carry two people, Kimberly is it safe for me to carry our wounded friend?"

"Yes, I can walk" Kimberly said.

Kent thought for a second then looked at both Kimberly and her mother again "Listen Kimberly I have a Battlebot myself."

"Really what type?" Goldsupervena asked excited.

"Um, it's the model known as the Magic Fighting Battlebot. These models fight with magical powers. Mine like yours is the most strongest Magic Fighting Battlebot but is weaker than Goldsupervena" Kent said.

"Oh, my gosh! He has Lightspirit the one and only God Power Magic wielding Battlebot" Flower shouted.

"Good that is good, Lightspirit has the Heaven's Heal ability which heals fatal wounds and minor injuries on people" Moonshine said recalling all of the Battlebot models and names.

"Kent we have to get Lightspirit to heal Flower does he have powerful Magical attacks?" Kimberly asked.

"Yes, he does follow me" Kent said.

"Kimberly please…I just lost my son and I don't want you to be lost as well" Kimberly's mother said once more pleading her daughter to call it quits.

"Sorry mother, someone has to take a stand, I'm going to save the USA! Now I'll come back safe and sound!" Kimberly said.

Kimberly's mother hung her head down in defeat "Your brother's courage is powerful in you. Well just come back in one piece and alive."

"I will mother" Kimberly said hugging her mother.

Kimberly's mother hugged her last surviving child firmly and began crying.

"I'll be back," Kimberly said with deep sorrow in her voice.

Goldsupervena stepped forward and bowed to the saddened mother "I will protect her. I won't let anything happen to her."

Kimberly's mother nodded "Thanks."

"Not a problem, Moonshine and I will take care of her," Goldsupervena said.

"You've pulled the words out of my mouth old friend" Moonshine said.

"Next stop Kent's house!" Kimberly shouted.

"Right, Lady Kimberly" Goldsupervena said saluting her.

Behind them Kimberly's mother looked at the sky and prayed "Please god please watch after her."

The five heroes went onwards towards Kent's house.

"Terror from this moment on I have declared war, prepare to fall!"

The five friends continued on their journey.

Chapter 7
Railbuster Returns

Terror the Assassin was worried. Railbuster his fateful second-in-command never took this long to capture an item. Railbuster returned and the wounds on him made Terror gasp out. Railbuster returned with a hole in his chest, a chopped off hand, and a nasty Magicsaber beam blast.

"**RAILBUSTER** What happened to you?" Terror asked.

"Milord, the girl she didn't give me the blade. I tried to kill her twice but my brother being the stubborn person around ladies like her was protecting her at every turn" Railbuster said.

"So, the girl...is it true that she is peaceful?" Terror asked.

"Yes and no. She looked like she was about to give me that Magicsaber of hers but my brother told her that the big Battlebot she saw was me, after that well she refused saying that she'd rather die than help evil even if she's peaceful."

Terror stalked his ground "So, we've failed to capture the Magicsaber of Light. That's a desperate loss to us. We need that so we can be invincible. So who done these horrible wounds on you? And does she have the Magicsaber of Light?"

"Yes, oh mighty Terror, in fact the legend is true she is the one and only person to wield the Magicsaber of Light. If she were to have hit me directly she could've killed me. So my wounds were from three people, the girl's boyfriend whom stabbed me in the back with his Magiclance which made this hole in me, then as I went to slice the boy's head off my brother makes his move which cuts off my hand, then as if I was too far away the girl, Kimberly fires from afar. Believe me I would've had four wounds had it not been the fact that I reflected a Magic Snipping Rifle blast back at the person who did it. It almost killed her I think she broke her legs and twisted her arm by the surprised fall she took. As I went to destroy her then that unicorn sent a magical beam which canceled my Magicsaber beam out."

"Enough with your story. So Kimberly's the one that can defeat me. Then send all units to attack her at every turn."

"Yes, Milord soon that blade will fall into your hands" Railbuster said.

"Yes, but now we need to kill the girl too, she is the one that can wield the blade" Terror said.

"Okay, but I'm wounded."

"Well then get repaired and then send out my orders I'll need you around here."

"Ooohhh my back. Oh as you command Milord"

Under the twenty-four seven-hour guard the captive marines looked at one another.

"Sergeant Bash when can we escape?" one asked.

"It's not time right now. We need to know if Magic Force can defeat Terror" Sergeant Bash said.

"How many battles Sergeant?"

"About three battles."

"Oh, pray that Magic Force can defeat them, so after Magic Force wins three battles we make an attempt?"

"Yes, but try to start digging right now but it's not time to escape" the sergeant said

The sergeant wanted everyone out but he knew Terror was too strong and would easily notice an early escape.

Chapter 8
Lightspirit

It took a while to get to Kent's house. Kimberly was tired out but Moonshine urged her to continue. Kimberly thought of the ways, how could she control the whole entire army of Magic Force. She needed some Generals and Commanders to help her. She knew Goldsupervena was a war hero and so was Moonshine. Kimberly tripped over a tree root and fell face first into the dirt. Goldsupervena helped his mistress up.

"You okay Lady Kimberly?" he asked.

"I'm okay," Kimberly said brushing off the dirt from her skirt and shirt.

Kent knocked on the door of his house.

Kent's father came out.

"Kent your safe" he said.

"Yes, father I'm safe" Kent said.

"Kent you've made us so worried about you" Kent's mother said.

"Sorry, I had to drop off my girlfriend at her house first then we decided to come here and get Lightspirit" Kent said.

"Girlfriend?" Kent's sister asked.

"Someone who is very close and is the opposite sex for a boy" Kent's mother said.

"So where is this girlfriend of yours Kent?" his sister asked.

Kimberly walked up to Kent.

"Um here she is" Kent said grabbing onto Kimberly's hands.

Kimberly looked at Kent she didn't know what was going on.

"What a cute girl you have Kent, whats her name?" Kent's mother asked.

"Kimberly" Kent said.

Kimberly closed her eyes at the sound of her name being called out.

"You sounded just like my brother right then" Kimberly said.

Kent's father looked at Kimberly and said "The sweet brown hair and pale white skin."

"I beg your pardon?" Kimberly asked.

"Nothing Kimberly, so you're the young lass that has taken my son's heart that's nice so how old are you?"

"Um thirteen" Kimberly said.

"Oh you're the same age as Kent that's nice" Kent's mother said.

"Oh she's cute" Kent's sister said hugging Kimberly.

"Uh Kent can we get Lightspirit and continue towards Terror's base?" Kimberly asked.

"Did I just hear her say Terror?" Kent's sister asked.

"Yes" Kent said.

"Kimberly you must be brave but without the Magicsaber of Light you can't win with just the two of you" Kent's father said.

Kimberly sighed, "I am the weilder of the Magicsaber of Light." She pulled out the Magicsaber's handle and enlightened it. The Magicsaber of Light came to life responding to her touch.

Kent's father looked at the blade "Well I'll be the Magicsaber of Light, with it you'll stand a chance against Terror. Hm, but it's only you and Kent, you don't have an army."

Then Kent's mother noticed the army.

"Well they have an army"

Kent's sister watched one of Kimberly's Magic Troopers on Swift's back come up and salute her.

"Hello Flower, how can I help you" Kimberly asked.

"Um not to be a bother to you Kimberly but, we need to get going" Flower said.

"Of course" Kimberly said.

"If I could help Kimberly, I studied about Magic Force years ago so I'm coming with you. My name is Professor Strike. I could teach you everything about Magic Force" Kent's father said.

"You sure about coming with us?" Kimberly asked.

"Yes"

"Okay, Kent get Lightspirit and then were out of here"

"Yes, Kimberly"

"Lightspirit!" Kent shouted.

A half cheetah half human Battlebot came out. It had the whole entire body of a human but it had cheetah characteristics on him.

"You called Master Kent? Lightspirit asked.

"Yes, were going to attack Terror and we have an emergency!" Kent said.

Lightspirit nodded he knew what emergency meant and walked out. He noticed Kimberly who was gasping at him. He caste a good look around him. Then he noticed Goldsupervena.

"Goldsupervena, I thought you were fighting in the US military and why are you near the horn horse?" Lightspirit asked.

"What did HE JUST SAY?" Moonshine asked anger quickly filling in her.

Goldsupervena held up his fist to silence his maddened unicorn friend "I was but Tommy gave me to Lady Kimberly and this is Moonshine, I know. I know, that Battlebots aren't supposed to be friends with a unicorn cause of our differences but Moonshine and I are exceptions," Goldsupervena said.

"Oh, sorry Moonshine forgive the preacher" Lightspirit said.

"Apology accepted!!!"

"Okay so where is the patient?" Lightspirit asked.

"On Swift" Kimberly said.

"Oh, and are you the leader of this army? Oh sorry, let me introduce myself, I am Lightspirit" Lightspirit said.

"I am Kimberly and I'm the leader of Magic Force, my friend Flower has two broken legs, a twisted arm and a bullet wound can you cure her?" Kimberly said.

"Yes, by the power of the Gods, I Lightspirit will cure a victim" Lightspirit said.

"Gods? I thought there was one God" Flower said.

"Um, if it helps Lightspirit believes in many gods. This is how he gets his magical powers" Goldsupervena explained.

"Oh that makes since" Flower said looking at Goldsupervena.

"Well Kent help her down" Professor Strike said.

"Right" Kent said as he picked up Flower and placed her down on the ground where she collapsed unable to stand.

"Hm, you are in a dangerous state here let the Gods help you up. HEAVENS HEAL!" Lightspirit said as he spread his paws wide. Yellow light shown from the sky and gently shown off Flower. Kimberly watched as the light engulfed her friend and when it settled, Flower stood on two legs and the bullet wound was gone. Flower stared at Kimberly as well both girls watched as the light faded away.

"Well I see everything is okay now, the Gods have done their job today" Lightspirit said.

"Lightspirit come with us, we'll need your amazing healing powers to fight" Kent said.

"As you command"

Kimberly stopped as they got near the woods and began to relax.

"Goldsupervena, Moonshine could you two be my generals?" Kimberly asked as she sat down on a log.

Goldsupervena and Moonshine walked up to Kimberly.

"Looking for good Generals now are we?" Moonshine said.

"Yes, you see, I never had any military experiences so..." Kimberly said looking at the Battlebot and unicorn.

"So you're looking for ones that have military experiences," Goldsupervena said finishing Kimberly's sentence.

"Yes" Kimberly said.

"Well, your looking at the right people for the job" Moonshine said.

"We know a lot about war, why are you bringing up this subject may a certain Battlebot ask?"

"Well Goldsupervena as you know an army needs a strong leader, but I'm peaceful and don't know anything about war. So I figure I need generals to help me out," Kimberly said.

"You thought right then, sure, Goldsupervena and I can be your generals" Moonshine said.

"Good, well have to divide the units by half, Moonshine will you accept all myth units and flying units?"

"Yes, I will. I will be the general of Magic Force's myth units and flying units," Moonshine said.

"Then Goldsupervena gets the ground forces. How's that?" Kimberly asked.

"That sounds like a great idea!" Goldsupervena said.

Kent, his father Professor Strike, Flower, and Lightspirit slept soundly.

"Magic Force awaken!" Kimberly shouted.

"Oh, uh, Kimberly, I was taking watch" Flower said innocently and pretending to be awake.

Goldsupervena noticed that no one else was waking up so he banged a bell Moonshine had given him.

Everyone woke up with fright.

"What is it Kimberly?" Professor Strike asked shocked.

"Um, I've nominated the generals" Kimberly said.

"Who are the generals?" Lightspirit asked.

"General Goldsupervena and General Moonshine"

"That's a great idea, making the ones who have been in war,

generals that's smart thinking" Kent said.

Kimberly watched as the rest of Magic Force cheered them on.

"Oh yeah, we also need commanders, a preacher and a professor" Kimberly said.

"Okay and let me guess who the preacher is" Lightspirit said.

"Go ahead" Goldsupervena said.

"Me right"

"Yes, Lightspirit you are our preacher about God" Kimberly said.

"Oh, you mean the Gods"

"Sure whatever you say"

"Okay and what about the Commanders?"

"I figured you'd say that Moonshine. Kent is the Commander of our Magic Cavalier units, and Flower is our Magic Trooper commander"

"Gee, uh thanks Kimberly" Flower said.

"Thank you Kim" Kent said placing his arm around her shoulder.

"I guess I'm the Professor" Kent's father said.

"Of course Professor Strike."

Kent's father shrugged "Well okay."

Kimberly lay down on the ground near the fire. Kent sat next to her *what a beauty* he thought. He looked at her for a long time before falling asleep himself. The now nominated General, Goldsupervena watched the camp area for Terror's troops.

Chapter 9
The First Battle

Terror the Assassin watched Railbuster. His Battlebot companion was taking so long to repair. The Assassin wondered if he shouldn't have sent Railbuster to retrieve the Magisaber of Light. Terror looked to his troops in his area.

"Troops, we have found the Magicsaber of Light. It is found in the hands of a young girl named Kimberly. Your job is to kill her at all costs. From this day on, The Machine Assassin Empire will defeat Magic Force. This declares war on Magic Force! Now is there anyone in the first military troop addition that will not obey my orders?" Terror asked.

One electric drone thought of it before raising his hand. Terror's mechanical ripping claws made short work of the unlucky drone.

"Anyone else?" Terror asked.

Looking at their fallen comrade none raised their hands not wanting to be the victim of Terror's dangerous mechanical ripping claws.

"Thought so, now listen my first army division, I need you to go and try to kill the girl first. Railbuster would be joining you and leading you but as you can see, Railbuster is dreadfully wounded so I will put you all in the toughest commanders. They will most likely be loyal to me. Now go, Electro the Electric Drone will be your leader go and destroy the girl and capture the Magicsaber of Light" Terror told his forces. Every one of Terror's forces ran out all wanting to be in the first trooper division. Terror noticed most of his forces out of five thousand going in the trooper division.

"Halt only one thousand per division at first" Terror said.

"But sir" another assassin drone complained.

"You heard him," Railbuster said.

"But sir" the drone asked again.

Terror's ripping claws struck the drone as Railbuster drew his Magicsaber.

"Any objections? You will do as Milord Terror commands."

"Okay mercy Lord Terror" the assassin drone said.

Terror released him "Good, now that your hearing is better go guard the prisoners."

Sergeant Bash looked to his fellow troops. US Troops looked at the ground as he urgently began digging.

"Now is the time to escape" Bash said.

"Yes, but wouldn't Terror notice?" a soldier asked.

"Yes, he would but we can fortify this position" Bash said.

"Good, idea and help Magic Force" a trooper named Sea said.

"Yes, he can't hold us for long" another troop agreed.

"He can and he will" Terror said coming in the room.

All talking stopped "So trying to escape?"

"No sir" a soldier said.

"Well, that's good cause if you do I will notice and catch you" Terror said.

Sea noticed Terror's murderous voice.

"Magic Force will stop you!" she shouted.

"Oh and you and what army?" Terror asked.

"I just know Magic Force eke" Sea began as Terror brought his claws to her neck.

"Put her down" Sergeant Bash said.

"Okay" Terror said flinging Sea into the ceiling.

"You murderer" Sea said as she hit the ground.

Terror looked at Sea and saw the resemblance of Tommy in her.

"Are you perchance his sister?" Terror asked.

"No you jerk, his sister is seven years younger than he is" Sea said as she aloud Bash to help her up.

"Goldsupervena should've killed Railbuster," a trooper said.

"Ah, but he didn't" Railbuster said while walking in with a repair drone repairing him.

"Oh-my-gosh" Sea mumbled disgusted by looking at the wounds on Railbuster.

"Oh, Goldsupervena wouldn't have done that much damage to his own brother" Bash said.

"These are nothing but my brother has definitely crossed the lines! He helped that young girl survive. He will do it again but he's my brother and will be destroyed!" Railbuster said.

Terror looked at Sea mystified.

"You, there you wouldn't be by any chance, Tommy's girlfriend?"

"I would be his girlfriend, I know one thing about his sister that you don't know. Even though she isn't a soldier as we are, she knows vows. And she problobly might've vowed that one-day to kill you. And I also vow that. If I get out of here you better watch your back!" Sea said.

"Curse you human, you can't do anything to me or Terror not at the stage you are in!" Railbuster said.

Terror stopped and looked at Sea.

"She means it Railbuster but you're right she can't do anything but his sister can"

The assassin left the area with Railbuster following him with one turn, Railbuster turned to look at the captives then left.

"Good one Sea, good bluff" a trooper said.

"She wasn't lying, she meant it" Sergeant Bash said.

Sea nodded "That Assassin Drone is going to get it, he'll fine a bullet or a Magicsaber in his chest. Kimberly, we'll see who gets the Assassin first. For I know you will vow to bring your brother's killer to justice" Sea said.

"Leave that to Kimberly, she has a better weapon to combat Terror" Bash said.

"What did I say that? I said things evilly why me?" Sea asked herself.

"It's because you are angry and you have the right to be angry, but let the killing to Kimberly, she's his sister" Bash said.

"Right I see exactly what you mean, but I really do mean that I will kill Terror myself" Sea said.

"And I do to, I want to kill that Assassin Drone but he's guarded well" Bash said.

"Right, so are we going to fortify this place?"

Bash grinned, "Definitely, one thing, drones are not very smart, they left us armed and were in a weapon stash."

Every soldier turned and grinned as they saw what Bash meant.

"Just wait until tomorrow night," Bash said.

Electro and his men made it to the forest during the dark night. Kent was patrolling Magic Force's part of the forest. His girlfriend, Kimberly was sound asleep. General Goldsupervena as Kent observed while watching the general never slept. Kent looked around and saw Electro's forces.

"Search every area the girl must be caught and killed. Terror's orders" Electro said.

Kent leapt on Swift and road into camp.

He tapped General Goldsupervena.

The general looked at Kent.

"What is it Kent? Danger?"

"Yes, general, Terror's forces are here" Kent whispered.

Goldsupervena wasted no time.

"Arise the forces" Goldsupervena said.

Kent nodded and aroused his units. Kent gently picked Kimberly up.

"Wait I'm not ready to go to school" Kimberly said.

"Um, Kimberly sorry to break it to you but we are involved in a war" Flower said.

Kimberly opened her eyes and saw herself in Kent's arms.

"Oh" Kimberly said as Kent placed her down.

"Listen, Milady, the enemy is among us" Goldsupervena said.

"Oh, then I will walk into plain view of Terror's Forces."

"Terror wants you killed!" Kent said.

"I know, now listen, while I walk into plain view, General Goldsupervena with the help of General Moonshine's magical abilities will position my forces around the trees behind the enemy forces. Once their commander orders an attack on me and I reflect the blast, this will be the single to counter attack fire at will then" Kimberly said.

"Good idea" Flower said as General Goldsupervena went right to work.

Kimberly knew she was in trouble but also knew that it was her time to shine and the joke once more was on her foe's forces.

Electro stopped as he saw the girl.

"Well this is the girl is it not?" Electro asked.

"This girl surrendered herself to us. She knows what we want to do with her," an Assassin Drone said.

"Well let's end it now, any last words?" Electro said.

Kimberly shook her head "Well five, let me join my brother."

"I'll make your death quick then" Electro said raising his hand.

Kimberly watched him as he stopped.

"I.I.I. I'm a drone loyal to Terror but I can't kill a beautiful girl" Electro said.

"Some Commander you are" the Assassin Drone said.

Electro looked at him "You! How dare you say that, okay I'll kill her shock her troops!"

Immediately the troops opened fire on Kimberly. Kimberly

watched as the electrical blast drew near her. *This really will kill me* she thought.

Electro watched as the electric blast drew near his victim. Then at the last possible movement, Kimberly reached for the Magicsaber of Light and reflected the blast back at the stunned drones. Electro backed away from the blade knowing that it could destroy him in one blow.

Kimberly watched as eight electric drones fell destroyed by their own blast.

"Blast, now I have to kill you!" Electro said.

"Come on do you think I'd surrender myself to you this easily? Boy you were fooled, listen, **MAGIC FORCE!**" Kimberly shouted.

General Goldsupervena returned her call "Were coming **MAGIC FORCE!**"

Magic Troopers under their leadership of both General Goldsupervena and Flower opened fire upon Terror's Forces.

Twenty drones fell under Flower's and General Goldsupervena's Magic Troopers blast. Fifteen more were taken out by Kent's Magic Caviler group. Magic Force charged firing their weapons catching the enemy completely off guard. Flower's snipping gun proved fatal to any drone that it shot. Goldsupervena used his Magicsaber, twirling it expertly in his windmill fashion. Drones that were near him were instantly destroyed, and flung into the air. Moonshine's magical powers claimed the lives of many drones. Most drones tried to get away from the advancing force firing away. They looked at an advancing robot.

"Railbuster thank goodness help us," the drones shouted as the robot drew near.

The drones watched as the robot came into view.

"Sorry I work for your enemy" the robot said.

"What Railbuster a traitor? Kill him!" Electro shouted.

"Sorry, I'm not Railbuster, I'm Lightspirit besides the Gods don't like traitors such as yourselves" Lightspirit said.

"What traitors, and oh-no, Terror is my leader and I must do what he orders!" Electro shouted.

"Then so be it! You've angered the Gods! Alas for my power, take this, Destructive Flame!" Lightspirit sarcastically said.

A powerful circling fire ability charged towards the enemies. Drones tried to retreat not wanting to feel the wrath of the angered Gods. The Fire attack hit the first row knocking down and melting drones. Electro fired his electric blast at Kimberly but the girl's Magicsaber of Light reflected his blast and neatly sliced threw an advancing Assassin Drone. Electro attacked Kimberly again this time he succeeded in shocking her but thanks to Moonshine's magical powers, it didn't cause any damage to her.

Kimberly easily shrugged of the Electric Drone's attack. Electro lifted his hand to strike Kimberly's head but her Magicsaber of Light found it's mark in his chest. Electro shrieked as the powers of light flowed through him and destroyed him.

The rest of Terror's Forces stopped their attack as they saw Electro fall. They retreated from Magic Force.

"Our first battle and our first victory!" Kimberly mumbled.

General Goldsupervena and General Moonshine walked up near their leader.

"Lady Kimberly what are we going to do with the ones that are retreating?" General Goldsupervena asked her.

Kimberly looked at her generals.

"If we pursue them. Most won't live to try to kill you another day" Moonshine said.

"If we don't then the whole entire army will live to try to kill you another day" General Goldsupervena advised her.

Flower took a look at a destroyed drone she had shot down then without tears in her eyes to Kimberly.

"War isn't pretty! I'm peaceful as you are Kimberly but I don't want us to be in slavery! So your decision is final!"

Kimberly nodded to her friend and her two generals "That's true let them retreat safely, I'm interested to see what they will be like if we ever met up again."

"Right but next time let's be on high alert" Moonshine advised.

"Okay, you said it"

"Good listening to us generals" Goldsupervena said.

"And friends" Flower added.

"May I ask why?" Kent asked winking at Lightspirit.

"Sure, America is united, America is strong, and America is a Democracy. I was raised in a Democracy! Therefore as my first act as Magic Force's leader, I Kimberly will make Magic Force also a Democracy!" Kimberly said.

"Power is in the people, good idea," Lightspirit said.

"Your saying that Magic Force's leader will be decided by the people and not the Magicsaber of Light's power?" Flower asked.

Goldsupervena looked at Flower and shook his head "No, the leader is automatically summoned by the Magicsaber of Light's judgment."

Professor Strike nodded "True, Kimberly is the one and true leader of Magic Force. However it is in Kimberly's blood, whoever is her child will be the next wielder of the Magicsaber of Light. Then her child's child will wield it and then…"

"Please stop" Kent begged.

"Oh sorry son got a little carried away."

Kimberly nodded in understandment "I get it I've started a heredity trend. However whatever the rules and laws of Magic Force, will totally come from the people."

"Oh, I get it" Flower said.

"Good now let's get some sleep."

"Can't argue with that logic," Moonshine said.

"Go ahead General Goldsupervena, go to sleep, I'll take another shift" Kent said.

"Sorry, Commander, but Battlebots can't go to sleep, were programmed to stay awake" Goldsupervena said.

"Well there's got to be a shut down button"
"There isn't" Lightspirit said.
"Okay I'll go get some sleep general"
"Good then I'll stay awake and guard this camp"
Goldsupervena watched as Kent and Swift knelt down to get rest.

Chapter 10
A Failed Attempt

Terror watched the remainder of his first trooper division. He looked shocked, how could a girl with four of her friends defeat such a huge army? He looked at the army and then to Railbuster whom was still not fully repaired. Railbuster nodded to his leader.

"What happened? How could a girl and four of her friends defeat a huge army?" Terror asked his men.

"Um, sir she wasn't alone, she had two more people with her a Magic Fighting model Battlebot, Lightspirit and a Professor" a drone said.

"Could it be that she's smarter than us getting two new people? It doesn't matter seven people is all she has, you should've destroyed them!"

"Um Milord forgive the interruption but the Magicsaber of Light has our enemy forces inside it. Kimberly could have launched the beginning of an army," Railbuster said.

"Oh, well what is the next army going to be in?" Terror asked.

"Well, in a fort sir" a drone said.

"They'll have to get in it to destroy our forces inside" Railbuster said.

"It is heavily equipped sir and most likely will survive any assault," a trooper said.

"Good the rest of you go to that fort" Terror commanded.

"Terror were under attack in the inside the prisoners are rebelling!" one of Terror's officers shouted.

"Railbuster lets see what is happening down there"

Sergeant Bash fired away at an advancing Assassin Drone. Sea fired her flamethrower at anything that drew near her.

"Terror's coming" Sea said.

"Cease fire men" Sergeant Bash said.

The firing soldiers stopped as Terror burst in.

"Think your clever human?" Terror asked.

"Yes, were more clever than drones. We heard that your forces were defeat…" Sea began.

An arrow flew threw the window and hit her instantly killing her.

Sergeant Bash looked at Terror.

"Wasn't me human, none of my people," the Assassin Drone quickly rammed Bash onto the ground and ran towards the window and looked down. Native Americans were firing arrows after arrows at the fort.

"Railbuster charge those natives!"

"Um ready but I'm still hurt Milord."

"Natives?" Sergeant Bash asked.

"Quickly use those Nuclear drones on them Railbuster!" Terror shouted.

"Right" Railbuster said.

Terror turned and saw his error, "I'll deal with those weapons Sergeant Bash."

"Oops" Bash mumbled.

Railbuster and his men rode outside of the dungeon, just as Terror destroyed all of the guns and ammunition it the dungeon with the Magicsaber of Darkness. The rest of the captive soldiers were forced to surrender their weapons.

The native American leader Jack Lateint new that his arrow missed his intended target as he saw his arrow hit a US troop killing her. He sighed and shook his head. Everyone in his forces saw the drawbridge open and out came Railbuster this time fully repaired. He was surrounded with thousands of Nuclear Drones.

Jack waved his hand "Fire Nutralisk!" and with those words, ten arrows flew at Terror's Forces. The arrows hit their targets but didn't stop the drones, which continued their march towards the natives. Railbuster smiled at them as his forces advanced on the Natives.

"Nice try but regular arrows don't harm robots!" Railbuster said as the startled natives started a retreat.

Jack shook his head he had made his retreat too slow and the enemy was advancing on them.

Jack watched ten of his men fall down instantly slain by the Nuclear Drones. Railbuster caught up behind the Nutralisk leader. Five Nutralisk soldiers flung themselves at Railbuster swords drawn.

Jack and his men ran deep into the woods and continued their retreat just as the five Nutralisk Soldiers were killed by Railbuster's blade.

Fifteen Nutralisk were killed in the attempt trying to fight against Terror's forces but Terror's forces didn't take any casualties. Jack right then new that Terror couldn't fall to the Nutralisk Force alone. Jack knew he must find at least an ally in order to defeat Terror, a very powerful ally one that could defeat Terror's forces for good.

Chapter 11
Confusion Alliance

Kimberly woke up quickly and looked into the blue sky. She quickly glanced at Kent whom was sleeping silently. She got up and quickly ran to the woods and near a stream. Kimberly generally knelt down and began to drink from it. She quickly got up and glanced around. She saw a Native American. In his hand was an arrow and in another was a gun. Kimberly didn't know what to do, she froze hoping that the native wouldn't kill her. The native raised his weapons and fired. Kimberly dived onto the ground the arrow missed her by an inch into the ground before her left leg and the bullet whizzed by her. The native raised his weapons again but this time General Goldsupervena rushed into the fry Magicsaber enlightened, he positioned himself in front of Kimberly. The native fired the arrow at Kimberly again but fired the gun at Goldsupervena. The arrow missed Kimberly's body but hit her skirt and pinned her on the ground. Kimberly sat up straight as Goldsupervena reflected the bullet right at the native. The native was taken back by surprise. Kimberly was struggling to remove the arrow, which pinned skirt and her to the ground. Her general Goldsupervena took command as his leader struggled.

"**MAGIC FORCE!!!**" Goldsupervena shouted.

Magic Force charged out of the trees and the native's forces came out as well. Both sides were confused until Goldsupervena took one native out with his Magicsaber. Both sides clashed violently. Magic Troopers took out many native troops but none of Native Americans took out any of Magic Force's men out. It wasn't long before the natives were defeated. Jack Latenit along with the remainder of his native force walked into the area. He was in time to see the first shots fired by the other native leader.

"Snipper!" Jack shouted as he came into view.

"Jack your just in time! We need to combined our forces together in order to destroy these enemies!" Snipper said.

Jack looked at the white armored troops then to his fellow natives.

"So this makes sixty-five men lost."

"You lost fifteen of us impossible! But to whom?"

"To Terror's forces"

Kimberly gasped "Terror's Forces?"

Jack looked at Kimberly questionably and drew a blade, walked up to her and placed his blade near her neck "You know him girl?"

Kimberly knew she was in no position to fight but she had to attempt to try to defend herself so she drew her Magicsaber of Light.

"I do know Terror! And I'll fight anyone loyal to him!"

Jack watched the young struggling girl questionably.

"How? You look like someone I know" Jack said.

Kimberly struggled to look at Jack "Maybe it's because my brother was Tommy!"

Jack gasped "Tommy" then he noticed Snipper placing an arrow to his bow and lowering his gun.

Jack stopped Snipper "Hold it Snipper this girl is Tommy's sister!"

"No she and her forces took out fifty of our men!" Snipper said.

Goldsupervena took action "Quite! You tried to kill Kimberly, I was only defending her."

Moonshine the Unicorn nodded her head.

"**Railbuster!**" Snipper said lowering his gun towards Goldsupervena.

Goldsupervena made a move to grip his Magicsaber and strike Snipper down right then but Moonshine took his anger for him.

"**Y.y.y. YOU LITTLE NATIVE! CAN'T YOU TELL THE DIFFERENCE BETWEEN THE EVIL RAILBUSTER AND THE GOOD GOLDSUPERVENA?**"

Jack backed away from the angered Unicorn. In his native culture it was against their religion to upset a unicorn. Kent tried to help Kimberly up but when he done so the arrow would rip threw Kimberly's skirt.

Kimberly struggled as Jack came towards Kimberly.

"This young lady is innocent Snipper, and I will protect her with my life" Jack said as he removed the arrow from Kimberly's skirt. Moonshine walked over to Kimberly and with her horn glowing repaired the ripped skirt.

Snipper glared angrily at Jack "Why do you protect her Jack, she along with most of her own people completely destroyed the natives! She has to pay"

"No, not this one, the USA military isn't cruel to us as they once were. This is a young girl, remember all members of the Nutralisk tribe are allied to the USA military! This girl is Tommy's sister. And this Battlebot is Goldsupervena the one good Battlebot you can trust from the USA!" Jack said.

Snipper lowered his weapons in defeat. "You win, Jack. Sorry for attacking you Kimberly, I thought you were just a person working for Terror."

Kimberly shook her head "I'm alright a little shaken up but to tell all members of this native tribe, my fellow friends and army troops are going to fight against Terror, we just won a battle with his forces last night!" Kimberly said.

Jack looked at Kimberly and smiled "So, your against Terror?"

Kimberly nodded "Yes, totally against him that evil pile of scrap metal excuse for a spider! I will fight him until the end. No make that Magic Force will fight him to that end!!!" Kimberly shouted.

Jack bowed to the young girl.

Snipper gasped "**JACK!**"

Kimberly and Kent looked at the Native leader questionably.

Jack looked at Snipper "It's okay, we've been allied to the world's greatest super power for ages, we can trust Kimberly cause she is the sister of Tommy. Kimberly please forgive Snipper. Will you accept our offer of alliance? You see we Nutralisk also are allied to the USA military. We all fear that if Terror is fighting against the US then he will start on us Nutralisk. We fought against him today and we lost that battle. His armored troops are too powerful to even dent with our powerful arrows. It is clear that we underestimated the enemy and are enemies to Terror as well." Jack said.

"Um Kent is this formal?" Kimberly asked.

Kent nodded "I think it's formal."

Goldsupervena answered her question.

"It is the Nutralisk way of offering an alliance. Kimberly, I am a Battlebot and have actually seen these people fight alongside us. They are ferocious fighters."

"Your saying…"

Moonshine answered for her Battlebot friend this time her voice was her normal tone "Listen, Kimberly, what Goldsupervena is saying is true. They are powerful fighters. What he is really trying to say is that the Nutralisk rarely get the chance to propose an alliance. When they do ask for an alliance the leader knows what he is doing."

Kimberly nodded "Okay, General Goldsupervena and General Moonshine, your points are taken thoroughly. Jack, I Kimberly of Magic Force gives you my word. I accept your offer of alliance!"

Jack got up and looked into Kimberly's eyes. Kent watched Jack but he knew that Jack was doing what was required in the Nutralisk culture to accept alliance. Apparently he had to look his allied partner's leader in the eye.

Kimberly felt that he was starring into her forever. Jack then spoke his words.

"Kimberly are you Magic Force's leader?"

"I.I.I I am" Kimberly stammered.

"Forgive her she isn't used to people starring at her" Flower said. "But she is the leader of this grand army."

Jack nodded and understood "Sorry, Lady Kimberly" the Nutralisk leader held up his hand and held her hand in his.

"Kimberly you have accepted an offer of alliance. Do you swear that you will never turn sides against us Nutralisk through out this war?" Jack asked.

Kimberly held the native's hand in her own hand.

"I Kimberly the leader of Magic Force swear that I will never switch sides during this bloody war against Terror's Forces!"

The two leaders watched each other.

Kimberly continued her speech "Jack and on your behalf do you swear that the Nutralisk will not turn on Magic Force? Will you see to it that if Magic Force falls then you will continue to fight this war?"

"Yes, Kimberly, let's hope that second part doesn't happen" Jack said.

Kimberly and Jack then shook hands.

"Alliance accepted Lady Kimberly of Magic Force!" Jack said bowing to her.

Kimberly nodded "Alliance Accepted, one more thing"

"Yes one more thing" Moonshine said.

Jack nodded "Go ahead"

"Is this alliance going to be temporary or permanent?" Kimberly said.

"Lady Kimberly, the Nutralisk Force is a permanent ally to Magic Force"

"Good, Magic Force and Nutralisk Forces, friends to the end" Kimberly said shaking Jack's hand.

The Nutralisk cheered on their leader as Magic Force cheered their leader on.

Jack went to speak with his Nutralisk members. Kimberly watched as her Native American allies built a fire. She smiled she had gotten herself an ally.

Moonshine walked over to her leader. Moonshine nudged Goldsupervena as the Battlebot made his way towards his leader.

"How was I?" Kimberly asked her generals.

Goldsupervena looked at her "You were brilliant"

Moonshine nodded "With the Nutralisk on our side we'd fine out how strong Terror's Force's are."

"This could work out to our advantage!" Goldsupervena said.

"How?" Kimberly and Moonshine asked.

Then Moonshine noticed her own question and banged her head against a tree noticing her own stupidity. Luckily Goldsupervena was dull and didn't notice the stupidity of the unicorn's question.

"Well for one thing Lady Kimberly, these are Native Americans, they can use the forest taking out many drones as he has. With the Native American allies on our side we can use the trees and other foliage as they can together we can be unstoppable" Goldsupervena said.

Kimberly nodded "That's right."

She watched as her allies along with her force danced in the Alliance Celebration. Kent placed his arm around her neck gently. She turned and looked at him.

"Kimberly, you look even more beautiful when a fire is blazing.

Kimberly blushed "Please…" she began.

Kent brought her towards him and kissed her on the lips. Kimberly stopped as she received the kiss. Kimberly brought her arms around him and kissed him back.

"Want to dance Kimberly?" Kent asked her as he brushed her hair gently.

Flower looked at her friend as she accepted Kent's request.

"Gee…I wish I had a boyfriend," she mumbled.

"Beautiful aren't they?" Moonshine said.

Flower jumped onto Moonshine's paw "Oh sorry General Moonshine."

"It's okay Commander. You okay?"

"Yes...I mean...well I'm happy for my friend...but I'm disappointed myself" Flower admitted.

Moonshine nodded "In time, you will find true love, Kimberly and Kent are a good couple."

Flower nodded in agreement with tears in her eyes "They are"

Jack Lateint looked at Flower. Snipper his second-in-command certainly noticed him. He looked to where Jack was starring. Then he noticed why and then mumbled to himself "Blonde girls...can't get away from em"

Jack walked up to Flower. Flower was laughing at jokes, Kent had to say about his horseback ridding adventures. Kimberly was every ounce the leader she should've been! She was everywhere talking and trying to learn the native's religion. Luckily Lightspirit was able to help with that problem. Like him the natives were polytheistic and all gods that they believed in were all unicorns.

"No wonder they know it's wrong to upset unicorns! They fear their Gods's power" Kimberly said.

Professor Strike sat besides Kimberly "Exactly, you see the powers of the unicorns are so unlimited. You should never ever upset one because they can put a million year curse on you" Professor Strike said.

Kimberly turned to Moonshine "Is that true?"

"Yes, I'm afraid it's true. There is only one Magic thing stronger than unicorns that we unicorns fear."

"What thing is that?"

"Well...Its the Magicsaber of Darkness, you see that Magicsaber feeds on the negative thoughts that are in you and becomes more stronger" Professor Strike said.

"Oh...Can the Magicsaber of Light do the same thing?" Kimberly asked.

"Only on the positive thoughts" Professor Strike said.

"Oh" Kimberly said.

Flower looked into the fire and smiled at her friend she was exactly what Flower had accepted a powerful but yet peaceful leader. She knew Kimberly hated war but she declared war on Terror to save the US and will see to it that it would be in peace again.

She felt a hand on her shoulder and turned frightened to see the Nutralisk leader.

"Sorry I didn't mean to startle you miss" Jack said.

Flower noticed that Jack was about her age maybe a bit younger. She shook her head "It's okay, I'm easily startled."

Jack looked into her blue eyes "What beautiful eyes."

Flower blushed and turned to see if Moonshine was using her magical powers to get the Native American's kind words.

With one headshake in the direction of no from the Unicorn, Flower knew that it was against the unicorn's magical rules to make people fall in love. Flower looked deeply into Jack's eyes.

"Thank you"

"No problem, hey Flower are you friends to Lady Kimberly?"

"Yes, in fact I'm her childhood friend, her boyfriend is that boy you see with her. I'm just sad since I don't have a boyfriend..." Flower said.

Jack gripped Flower's hand and kissed it.

"You are so wonderful" Jack said.

Flower stopped blushing "You like me?"

"Of course I do, say how old are you?"

"I'm twelve sir, Kimberly is five months older than I am, so she's thirteen years old" Flower said. "How old are you?"

"I'm thirteen" Jack said.

"Pretty young for a Nutralisk Leader" Snipper said interrupting the two.

"Snipper I was going to kiss her" Jack said.

"I guess Snipper and you aren't good friends," Flower said blushing at the words kiss her.

"He and I are good friends but we have some arguments but mostly he understands what I do"

"Sorry, but it's true you're the youngest person ever to lead the Nutralisk Force" Snipper said.

"Oh" Flower said as Kimberly came over.

Flower looked at Jack "It's been nice talking to you"

Jack nodded "Same here Flower and if you're lonely Snipper and I are always here to cheer up girls that are feeling lonely"

"It's our job as allies to cheer everyone on" Moonshine said.

"That's what being allies means," Goldsupervena said.

"Oh, Goldsupervena, your brother is as evil as ever he took out five of our men out within one blade stroke" Jack said to the Battlebot.

"Hmm. Remind me to defeat him for you then. I can defeat him"

"Sure you can Goldsupervena you're the strongest Magicsaber Fighting Model Battlebot" Snipper said sarcastically encouraging the Battlebot.

"That's actually true" Moonshine said.

"Oh" Snipper said disappointed in himself.

Goldsupervena nodded "Thanks for the support Moonshine, well anyway I pledge to defeat my brother no matter the cause!"

Kimberly, General Moonshine, General Goldsupervena, Jack Lateint and Snipper sat around while everyone else on the two allied forces danced and sang together, talking about their next move.

"As I said earlier today, our Nutralisk forces won't be able to do much good against these drones" Jack said.

"Oh dear" Kimberly said.

"Then I suggest that you upgrade your arrows" Moonshine suggested.

"How?" Snipper asked.

"Something humans call fire you just put fire on your arrows and fire them like regular arrows" Moonshine said.

"Be sure not to burn yourselves in the process" Goldsupervena said.

The two allied force leaders laughed at the Battlebot's words.

"I'm not kidding, did I ever to you the time when Moonshine had a burnt paw by a fire arrow?"

Moonshine looked embarrassed for the second time that day.

"You Battlebots always remember those embarrassing days. Anyways he's right. Fire Arrow burns are painful and a great destructor to robots, and Drones."

Lightspirit smiled at the unicorn "Is that a scar on your paw Moonshine?"

"Yes, it burnt like the dickens"

"She looked like she was in pain right then too" Goldsupervena said.

"And what did you do to help Moonshine, Goldsupervena?" Jack asked.

"I dumped Ice cold water on her," Goldsupervena said.

"More like apple cider" Moonshine mumbled just loud enough for the leaders to here.

Kimberly burst out laughing, "Oh boy, Moonshine when was this?"

"When Goldsupervena and I were very young and we didn't get along with each other then" Moonshine said.

"It was an honest attempt to put out the fire that was on your paw" Goldsupervena said.

"That was the most embarrassing day of my life burnt by a fire arrow on my paw and then some big Battlebot dumped apple cider on me," Moonshine said.

"Well, it's good to see you and General Goldsupervena getting along now" Kimberly said.

"True, Goldsupervena learnt his lesson of dumping apple cider on me"

"For the last time I thought it was water"

"Yes it was an honest attempt, and I forgave you after Tommy had to give me a bath trying to get rid of the apple cider smell"

Kimberly smiled "I guess even Battlebots make mistakes don't they Goldsupervena?"

"Yes, pouring apple cider on Moonshine was not a good idea. Another mistake I did was running into a electric power line."

"I had to free him from being shocked to death note this was when we were getting along" Moonshine said.

Kimberly nodded just as Kent burst ran in.

"Oh Kent, Goldsupervena and Moonshine have just told their most embarrassing moments" Kimberly said.

Kent smiled at Kimberly "That's great."

Kimberly smiled and enlightened her Magicsaber. The Magicsaber of Light came to life sending out two more units. A hover tank only it used magical powers to hover on the ground. It had a huge tank nozzle. In the second came out another trooper unit, this unit was like a Magic Trooper but instead of a Magic Snipping Rifle, it held a Magicsaber.

"A Magic Tank" Goldsupervena said to Kimberly looking at the hover tanks.

"And one of your new trooper units. It's what you are considered on the ground Kimberly, you and this trooper are Magicsabermen or Magicsaberwomen on your case" Moonshine said.

"Wow others like me and Goldsupervena" Kimberly said.

"Actually I'm a Battlebot" Goldsupervena corrected.

"Correct again."

Kimberly didn't watch what happened next the Magicsaber of Light sent out three more beams at Moonshine. The beams instantly hit Moonshine.

Moonshine began to repeat special voice sayings.

"Are you okay?" Goldsupervena asked her.

"Yes. Why wouldn't I be?"

"Well um you rolled into the fire"

"YOW!" Moonshine shouted.

Kimberly watched shocked not knowing what to do for Moonshine she was on fire.

"Put the fire out Moonshine" Kent shouted looking at Kimberly's shocked form.

"Goldsupervena you know what to do" Moonshine said.

"Um, we didn't pack any apple cider" Goldsupervena said.

"Get water!" Moonshine shouted.

"Oh okay" the towering Battlebot ran to the water's edge and scooped up water in a huge bucket and came with it.

Lightspirit walked into the area and saw Moonshine. He sighed, "Well let's put out that fire. Poseidon's Wrath!"

Lightspirit shot out a terrifying water attack. The blast surrounded Moonshine and dumped water all over her. When the water stopped moving, Moonshine was standing her ground with the flames completely out.

"Are you okay?" Kimberly asked recovering from her shock.

"Yes, thank you Lightspirit" Moonshine said.

"I got the water!" Goldsupervena said.

"Wait don't..." Moonshine tried to warning Goldsupervena.

PLUSH! Goldsupervena dumped the water on the unicorn.

"Oh it's out. Sorry Moonshine you could've warned me"

"Apology accepted and I tried to warn you ahead of time" Moonshine said.

"Well what happened?" Kimberly asked still recovering from shock.

"The three white blast hit me and I believe they are to form your myth units" Moonshine said.

"I must be seeing things I see three unicorns," Goldsupervena mumbled as he rubbed his eyes.

"Three?" Snipper asked.

Kimberly looked at Moonshine, "He's right, I guess Magic Force gets unicorns on their side"

Moonshine nodded "Plus Dragons, and Hydras" Moonshine said.

Kimberly jumped "Dragons? Hydra?"

"Ah, Greek mythological creatures. What a clever thought" Lightspirit said.

"Very powerful, that Magicsaber of yours Kimberly gave me the power to summon myth creatures," Moonshine said.

"Oh" Kimberly said.

Just then silence followed after those words. Kent raced into the camp on Swift's back.

What's up Commander?" Goldsupervena asked.

Oh Lady Kimberly, General Moonshine and General Goldsupervena we've got trouble. Enemies are lining up in a straight line they are coming this way," Kent answered calmly.

Jack looked at Kimberly and said to her "This is quite unsuspected of them."

"This is the second time they did this luckily Kent was able to spot them again" Kimberly said.

"Okay so we can expect this to happen many times so what's the battle plan ally?" Jack asked.

"Yes, well…since my force can fight them off we will hold them off. Meanwhile get your fire arrows ready and then together we will ambush the enemy" Kimberly said to the Nutralisk leader.

"Okay fight using fire arrows good plan, you think you can hold them off?" Jack asked.

"We can! We defeated them yesterday"

"Becareful" Jack said.

"She always is, just get those fire arrows ready if you want to be a helpful ally to restore the USA" Goldsupervena said.

Jack saluted the Battlebot "Right away sir" the Nutralisk leader ran to give out his orders.

"Listen Nutralisk let's make some fire arrows. Now our arrows as we know are weak and won't cause damage to Terror, but thanks to the wisdom of General Moonshine of Magic Force we will be useful now."

Snipper nodded "Let's make some fire arrows."

Meanwhile Kimberly followed Kent towards the enemy. They were lead by a very angry Nuclearbot named Greendeath.

"Kimberly of Magic Force surrender we got you where we want

you. Give us the Magicsaber of Light!" Greendeath said.

"Oh dear this again! **NEVER!** Not to a big scrap metal excuse for a spider he shall not get it! I'll fight you for it!" Kimberly called down. "Then face the true power of Terror! Charge them!" Greendeath shouted back with rage in his voice. No one insulted the Great Terror the Assassin to this Nuclearbot's face and ever survived. Terror's Forces charged Kimberly's forces.

"Fire!" Kimberly said.

Magic Force Magic Troopers, Terror's Nuclearbots, and Electric Drones fired on one another. Thanks to think armor and their adaptations, the Magic Troopers weren't easily killed by radiation as most troops were. However the armor proved to be little use with Electric Drones which one almost killed a Magic Trooper. He would've killed the Magic Trooper only he had a Magicsaber slice, which General Goldsupervena sliced through him.

"Thanks," the Magic Trooper said to his general.

"No, problem, hey Lightspirit we need to get the wounded out of here" the Battlebot general commanded.

"Right away. Get away from him you creepy Assassin Drone! Don't defy the Gods now! Oh well... I forgot you already did, Lighting Bolts of Zeus!" Lightspirit said as he gathered up Lighting bolts in his hands and throwing them towards the advancing Assassin Drones. The five Lighting bolts acted like powerful spears spearing the Assassin Drones and destroying them instantly. Lightspirit grabbed the wounded Magic Trooper and dragged him in the back of the line where Kimberly's Magicsaber of Light's newest ability came into play; it too could heal people. Her blade's powerful beam blast healed the Magic Trooper.

"There sure are a lot of them," Kimberly said.

"Blast it" Moonshine said as an Assassin Drone tried to climb up her. The unicorn General succeeded in throwing it off and onto another Assassin Drone the two drones fought each other. Ripping each other's wires sockets and bolts out.

"Arrgh, it's disgusting how Assassin Drones rip everything out of you" Flower shouted in disgust.

Kimberly nodded as she took out an Electric Drone with her Magicsaber of Light.

Greendeath fired his radiation at Goldsupervena. The Battlebot was completely immune to radiation blast and ignored the blast.

"Where are those Nutralisk?" Moonshine asked ducking a radiation blast.

Suddenly a fire arrow zipped out of behind a tree striking an Electric Drone bursting it on fire. The fire easily destroyed the drone. Greendeath was a fierce general but knew that fire could claim his life as well. However he knew he would have to destroy Magic Force and take the Magicsaber of Light to Terror or else be destroyed by Terror. Then as the startled drones recovered Magic Force and the Nutralisk Force threw out their war cries.

"**MAAAGGGIIICCC FOOORRRCCCEEE!** Charge em!" Kimberly shouted.

"**NUUUTTTRRRAAALLLIIISSSKKK!** Charge the drones remember our fellow friends!" Jack shouted.

The startled drones were taken by surprise. Two forces attacking them? Plus to the drone's eyes to make matters worse the two forces were allied to each other.

Many Nutralisk were ready to destroy the drones. Greendeath decided that it was time to play the coward.

"Come on men let's retreat into the fort we tried" Greendeath shouted.

Most drones nodded and started a retreat.

Magic Tanks came into view and blasted the enemies as they retreated. Magicsabermen sabered many that were too slow.

When it was clear to Kimberly and Jack that the enemy retreated fully only one thousand five hundred out of two thousand drones lay destroyed. Kimberly and Jack singled the enemy's retreat as a victory for both allied forces. Kimberly turned to Jack Lateint.

"Not a moment too soon. That went perfectly well," she said.

"Indeed I hear that they're going into a fort with three thousand men" Jack said.

"Make that with the remaining five hundred drones which includes Greendeath which makes three thousand five hundred" Goldsupervena said.

"Do we have any deaths?"

"Yes, ten of our Magic Trooper have died trying to hold off our position" General Goldsupervena said.

"Okay good show so do we take care of the enemy now?" Kimberly asked.

General Moonshine shook her head.

"The battles that we just fought over were troop to troop battles. But the enemy has the protection of the fort. We can to attack the fort but we'd lose casualties."

"Great… How many?"

"About maybe around fifty men"

"General Goldsupervena what can we do to take a fort?"

"Well sensing that the enemy is going to be sleeping, we should attack by night"

"That is way too dangerous" Flower said.

"No we need to use Myth units," Goldsupervena said.

Lightspirit laughed, "He's right, Myth units, I've always been wanting to attack with Myth units."

Moonshine nodded and got the message.

"Using myth units could be our greatest advantage let's attack Kimberly, our Myth units are going to show us their true power!" Moonshine said.

"Okay… Goldsupervena!"

"Yes, Lady Kimberly?"

"Guide us to the fort, make sure were out of reach" Kimberly ordered.

"As you command"

The two allied forces marched onward.

Chapter 12
Evil Learns

Terror looked at the slain body of Sea and knew that the arrow was meant for him. Terror watched as Railbuster came in. He admired Railbuster's strength but still found it hard to believe that Goldsupervena could defeat him. No other robot, and drone could ever destroy him with the exception of the Assassin of course.

"Did you kill the natives?" Terror asked him.

"Fifteen of them, they retreated once we came close and they relized that their arrows were not affecting our armies, Milord" Railbuster said.

Suddenly the telephone rang, Railbuster looked at Terror questionably.

"Yes, Railbuster I sent Commander Greendeath to eliminate Magic Force. Told him to call back once he did" Terror said reaching for the phone.

"Hello, Terror speaking whose this?"

"Commander Greendeath sir" Greendeath said.

"Well, I suppose that you are calling to say the girl is dead" Terror said.

"Terror please don't punish Greendeath. Greendeath tried to kill her, wish I could say I did but she defeated me!"

"Greendeath! I told you that I don't accept failure! When you report back to this base I'll destroy you for failing me!" Terror shouted.

"Please don't or you won't know this information," Greendeath said.

"Information?" Railbuster asked.

"It better be useful, or else," Terror warned.

"It is useful, I swear!" Greendeath said.

"Then tell us," Railbuster roared.

"Okay mighty Terror and Railbuster. The natives that you chased have allied themselves with Magic Force."

"Coward you ran away from Natives when they couldn't even harm you!" Railbuster said.

"Railbuster for once your wrong!" Terror said leaping up "You see Railbuster they have allied themselves with Magic Force, there can only be one native force that was allied to the US and that was the Nutralisk Force. They problobly will listen to their ally that has defeated us twice."

"Oh"

"Exactly what they did, the Nutralisk had Fire Arrows!" Greendeath said.

"Okay, calm down I won't kill you. That is good information now the Nutralisk Force can harm us. Are you inside the fort?" Terror asked.

"Yes, Mighty Terror" Greendeath said.

"If it falls retreat where you will meet a three thousand men army division. Whatever is left of your army can help our army survive. You and Destructor will lead this army is it clear?" Terror asked.

"Yes, and thank you mighty one" Greendeath said.

"Good now you're dismissed and let me know how that one battle goes," Terror said.

"Yes, sir" Greendeath said as he hung up.

Terror glanced to Railbuster "It's two against one now. It's getting out of hand."

"Indeed Milord looks as if that prophecy coming true"

"I have a great plan"

"Oh boy this I got to here"

"Here this Railbuster. I'll give you permission to defeat your brother when he comes here. I'll duel the girl," Terror said.

"Alone and how will you make her duel you?" Railbuster asked.

"By killing her friend," Terror said.

"I know it's a dumb question but which friend? She has gack!" Railbuster began as Terror grabbed his neck.

"I'm sick of your worrying, can't I go anywhere without you worrying?" Terror asked.

Railbuster tried to remove Terror's mechanical claws from his throat as he answered his master "Yes, you can I'm just asking a question."

"Let's see her childhood friend" Terror said throwing Railbuster to the side.

THUD! Railbuster slammed onto the ground and got up.

"Sorry I didn't mean to sound worried"

"It's okay, cause once Kimberly sees her friend slain right before her eyes she'll be filled with anger and I will kill her in her anger" Terror said.

"Well have to wait on that," Railbuster said.

"Sounds like a good plan partner?" Terror asked.

"Yes, Milord" Railbuster said "But what if you lose that round whose to give out orders around here?"

"I'm so glad you asked that. It is you Railbuster! You proven to me as a powerful leader! Therefore if I fall which it might not happen but if I do then you will take over" Terror said.

"Thank you Milord."

"Now let's see what happens oh yeah if we both fail and Greedeath is still alive then he will rule what's left of our empire" Terror said "He's as bad as you are" Railbuster admitted.

"Let's just go talk to the prisoners"
The two robots walked along the way.

Chapter 13
Fort Capture

Kimberly and her force along with the allied Nutralisk Forces followed General Goldsupervena. Along the way she ignited her blade. The Magicsaber of Light sent out three beams. Out of one beam came a mobile rocket launcher.

"The artery unit of Magic Force the Magic V3 Rocket packs a powerful punch it can take out ten men even though the missile didn't hit" Moonshine explained.

Out of the second beam came a flying unit. It was in shape of a triangle.

"Triangleship the bomber of Magic Force" Moonshine explained proudly.

The third beam hit Moonshine knocking her unconscious. General Goldsupervena had to carry the unconscious unicorn the whole entire way. By the time they reached the hill Moonshine awoke to find a washcloth over her eyes.

"I'm going blind!" Moonshine said.

"Quite Moonshine, were near the fort and are about to attack it the enemy appears to be asleep but won't be able to do so if you are making noise" she heard Lightspirit whisper.

She looked at Lightspirit whom was working on her as his patient.

"Hey General Goldsupervena, Lady Kimberly, she's awake" Lightspirit whispered.

"Thank you" Moonshine said.

"What happened to you? You were talking to me about the units we just received then you became unconscious" a very concerned Kimberly told the unicorn.

"The third beam caught me off guard" Moonshine said.

"So another myth unit?" Lightspirit asked.

"Yes, the Medusa!" Moonshine said.

"Don't look at her she can turn you into stone" Kent told Kimberly.

Moonshine shook her head "She'll turn the enemies into stone and she's a good archer her arrows are lighting arrows good against drones, and other mechanical stuff" Moonshine said.

"Good" Kimberly said to her team, "Let's give the enemy a welcoming party! Begin Moonshine release your Myth Units"

"As you command Kimberly" Moonshine said.

"General Goldsupervena are the Magic Rockets, and Magic Tanks in position?"

"Yes, Lady Kimberly at your command" the Battlebot general said saluting to her.

"Good"

Moonshine nodded and closed her eyes and spoke her phrase. Her horn glue white and the sky glue fiery red as she spoke the first phase.

"Come to me children of flame! Burn the enemies to the ground. Feast upon ones that are slow. Send your team the power they deserve. Children of Flame awaken once more!"

Out of the fire-red and dark skies came the pure white dragons with pink eyes. They glared at the fort bellow and waited for orders.

"Now for the Hydra, come to me you powerful beast. Feast upon the metal foes, as you will. Your hunger is never filled. Come on you million headed beast arise and help Magic Force and its allies win this fight!" Moonshine chanted. The fiery red skies turned to a dangerous dark sky and sent out a hydra. The powerful purple beast sat on two legs with a powerful tail and claws. It had one snake-like serpent head. It opened it's mouth in it were sharp teeth.

Kimberly gasped out to it, "Boy what big teeth you have!"

The hydra gave Kimberly a look and opened it's mouth wide open.

Flower trembled with fear imagining what the Hydra could do to her. Kimberly noticed her friend shaking dramatically "Concentrate Flower."

I am Kimberly Flower thought. She was concentrating she concentrated on the Hydra. She concentrated that the powerful foot claws sunk into her body. Then it lunges at her and succeeds in grabbing her. She could actually feel it's teeth rip her to shreds when she concentrated on that she fainted.

Kimberly looked at her fainted friend then to General Moonshine "You over did it."

"Sorry, I can recall it" Moonshine said sweet dropping.

"It's okay, um Goldsupervena, Moonshine, you two are my generals. Lead this attack, I'll see to Flower" Kimberly said.

"Okay, let's go" Goldsupervena said.

Jack looked at Kimberly "You sure?" he asked.

"Yes…I'm sure, go ahead and kill some for me"

"Okay then, Nutralisk move out" Jack ordered.

Thousands of Nutralisk men came out inside their tank Leaf Tanks so called for their shape, and Log Launchers along with Nutralisk Gliders followed in a military fashion.

Kimberly stood with Flower's unconscious form.

Moonshine looked to Kimberly "Medusa?"

"Yes, Moonshine then order the attack to begin," Kimberly said.

Moonshine nodded and with her horn glowing, chanted "Come on out my beautiful snake monster. Let those that see you turn into stone. Fire away at ones that don't. Help Magic Force once again!" Moonshine said.

A blue sky came over the unicorn and out stepped a score of Medusa! The half snake half human creature came out with a bow. General Goldsupervena and General Moonshine nodded as they thought off a plan.

"Goldsupervena I'm thinking we send the dragons to attack first" Moonshine said.

"Okay good distraction General, you're the myth unit general after all" the Battlebot general said.

"Okay then I'll send the hydra. Once the alarm has been spread I'll send the score of Medusa"

"Great, then after they go out to engage the myth units, I'll order my people to attack" Goldsupervena said.

"Sounds great Generals we will attack behind the trees" Jack and Snipper said.

"Good with luck this could be our easiest mission to bad Milady Kimberly isn't going to be here to lead it" General Goldsupervena said.

"She's concerned for Flower, I would be too but she's doing the best thing she is caring for her friend" Lightspirit said.

"The best things Gods all love is caring right Lightspirit?" Goldsupervena asked.

"Right, the gods all love a solid friendship one that will never fall" Lightspirit preached.

"Okay, go my dragons begin Operation Fort Destruction" Moonshine said.

Kimberly held Flower's body in her hands.

"Oh, I should've known not to let Moonshine summon the Hydra. Flower hates things that show its teeth at you" Kimberly said.

Flower came around as Kimberly poured ice-cold water over her friend's face.

"You okay?" Kimberly asked her.

"The Hydra it ate me!" Flower shouted.

"Oh-no your not eaten" Kimberly said.

Flower screamed and felt her body all over to make sure she was in one piece.

"It's okay your alive" Kimberly said.

Flower looked at Kimberly's concerned face.

"Kimberly you care for me?" Flower asked.

"Yes, you were my friend ever since we were babies. I'm concerned for you" Kimberly said.

"Thank goodness, when you said concentrate when the hydra was out I really did concentrate. I concentrated on its claws then it showed me it's teeth. I then concentrated it as if I was it's next meal. Ooohhh terrible" Flower said.

Kimberly placed a comforting arm around her friend "It's okay. I was nervous myself but leaders are not supposed to show fear otherwise the team will split" Kimberly said.

"So, it's okay if I show fear?" Flower asked.

"Off course now let's watch the battle"

"Okay!" Flower said as the two girls ran to Magic Forces, and the Nutralisk force's side.

It was dark and an electric Drone named Shocker was the first Drone in Terror's party to learn what lied ahead for him. Shocker watched as a dark cloud came over him. He glanced up.

"**D.D.D.DRAGONS!!!**" he yelled before the leading dragon blew out it's firey breath catching him on fire burning his metal to a deadly crisp. The drone had no time to fight back as the fire claimed it's life. Thousands of drones came into action but were powerless to fight against flying creatures that could breathe fire. Greendeath arose out of the dangerous power. He glanced at the nearest dragon and knew Terror must know about it.

"Greendeath to Terror do you copy?" he said.

Meanwhile Terror and Railbuster were waiting when Greendeath's message came.

"We hear you" Railbuster said.

"I'm under attack, by dragons, their obviously are on Magic Force's side and their burning us to shreds we can't harm them!" Greendeath said.

"Push on trooper I'll talk to the other troops about this" Terror said dismissing his troops.

"Right" Greendeath said he fired a radiation blast at a dragon. The radiation hit killing it instantly.

It didn't matter though the dragons had chased the men out. Another Nuclear Drone named Stealth watched as he retreated.

With a nod from it's general, the hydra stomped down the hill. Stealth was too busy running out that he ran into the Hydra. He noticed a shadow covering him. He turned and screamed out one word "SERPENT!" as the Hydra quickly ate the Nuclear drone. Suddenly Greendeath and his men ran out to engage the Hydra blasting away at the dragons whom were still faster than the blast. The Hydra just kept eating it's victims. Then Moonshine nodded and the score of Medusa charged.

"Snake women!" a nuclear drone shouted before turning to stone. Greendeath retreated back into the fort and let his forces fight against the odds of being frozen into stone and shot by the Medusa's arrows.

"Now, Nutralisk, now Goldsupervena!" Moonshine said.

"About time" Goldsupervena said not a big fan of waits.

Suddenly the enemy heard over the breathing sound of fire and the roaring sound of the Hydra two familiar war cries "MAAAGGGIIICCC FFFOOORRRCCCEEE!"

"NNNUUUTTTRRRAAALLLIIISSSKKK!"

With the war cries shouted out the battle was beginning.

Kimberly looked at her generals as they looked at her.

"Flower your okay!" Moonshine said.

Flower nodded and then looked at the Hydra which bit, slashed and ate it's way threw enemy waves not being hurt by the enemies radiation.

"I'm joining" Kimberly said.

"Me too" Flower said charging.

The two girls went right to work blasting and slicing away. The two wear like windmill blades, everywhere at once blasting and slicing.

Kent joined up and made them even more invincible.

Though casualties were low, Magic Force and it's allies the Nutralisk force were winning. Greendeath watched as ten of his drones followed their leader in a retreat. Kimberly and Flower stood looking at the fort, which was now itself in flames. The battleground was a disaster. Several drones lay burning, and destroyed. Kimberly came a little too close to a wounded Assassin Drone. It immediately launched itself onto her climbing up onto her neck.

"Help!" she cried.

Flower took one look at her childhood friend and gasped. She leveled her Magic Snipping Rifle to her eye and looked into it.

"Don't move Kimberly!" Flower called out.

Kimberly took one look behind herself and saw Flower lowering her weapon and she braced herself for impact. Flower took one last look before firing. Kimberly cringed watching the blast come near her. The blast hit the Assassin Drone full force destroying the drone.

"Thanks" Kimberly said while prying the Assassin Drone's arms from her neck.

"No problem" Flower said.

Kimberly and the rest of Magic Force went into a ruined fort. Moonshine easily repaired the fort with her magical powers.

"Kimberly the enemy is in full retreat," Kent told her.

Kimberly watched through out the night sky "Good tonight we rest."

Greendeath still had his little cell phone. He called Terror.

"Mighty one the fort has fallen and only ten of my men remain alive. Were just going to join up with the other group orders sir?"

Terror's voice sounded really evil as he replied "Capture the leader's friend and bring her to me."

Greendeath smiled at himself as he addressed his troops "When we get to our friend's forces we need to capture that Magic Trooper Commander and bring her to Terror.

"What about the leader?" a solider asked.

"It seems that Terror wants to kill her himself one-on-one" All of the soldiers found themselves in the other trooper group. "Greendeath! I guess we join forces to defeat Magic Force it's like old times" Destructor said not really thrilled in working with Greendeath. He knew that he had to carry out Terror's orders.

Out of thousands and thousands of units in the Machine Assassin Empire, only fifty of them were good. Most Assassin Drones were evil and loyal to Terror but only five of the Assassin Drones were good. Destructor was one of the good Assassin Drones.

"Indeed" Greendeath said.

The two commanders waited for the big push.

Chapter 14
Capture Complete

Kimberly woke fully feeling happy. Despite the war she and her friends fought in. Some Nutralisk were waking up. Others were already awake preparing a feast. Lightspirit looked at the sky as if he was just sensing something.

"What's up Lightspirit?" General Goldsupervena said.

The Magic Wielding Battlebot looked at the Battlebot General "I don't know, it seems like the Gods are sensing something. I can't make it out. I know now it's something bad. Lady Kimberly, something bad is going to happen today, something you won't like."

Kimberly looked around "The Gods are sensing something wrong?"

"Yes, I can't put my paw on it but I'll be finding out shortly" Lightspirit said watching the sky.

"Okay, um is it clear to march on now Goldsupervena?" Kimberly asked.

Goldsupervena didn't know what to do "I've never been a strong believer in God, or the Gods, but I do not know what to do, I guess it's safe to continue the war Lady Kimberly but you need to be cautious of Lightspirit's feelings"

"Right let's continue"

Kimberly led her forces to an opened field.

"Any word Lightspirit of the uneasy feeling you got from the Gods?" Kimberly asked.

Lightspirit looked at Kimberly "Not yet, it's still an uneasy feeling. I still don't like it and at the looks of things, the enemy is up to something."

Kimberly watched the Machine Assassin Empire's army.

"There sure are a lot of them," Kimberly said.

General Moonshine looked at the opposing army "Sure are, I'd say about three thousand and ten of them."

"Any signs of Greendeath?"

"No, I mean yes he's near a very dangerous looking Assassin Drone Commander."

Goldsupervena looked at the unicorn general and hopefully said to her "Terror finally?"

Moonshine shook her head "No, it's Terror's Assassin Drone commander when he's not leading an assault"

Goldsupervena gave a groan "Not Destructor"

Kimberly looked at the Battlebot general then to Lightspirit "Whose Destructor"

It was Goldsupervena whom answered her "Destructor is Terror's most experienced general, he never failed his master and neither has Greendeath until the last two battles."

Lightspirit looked at the sky then to Kimberly "These two commanders are here for something."

Kimberly looked at the enemy army "What are they up to?"

"That I do not know Lady Kimberly but please be cautious" Lightspirit reminded her.

"Right" Kimberly said as she positioned her men to fight against Terror's forces. The Nutralisk were waiting for the enemy to make the first movement.

Commander Greendeath looked at Destructor waiting for his command.

"There here sir" a sentry told Destructor.

"Good, now Greendeath what are mighty Terror's commands?"

Greendeath took one last look at their foe's army "To capture the leaders childhood friend and bring her to him."

"Then that's what we will do," Destructor said.

The Assassin Drone Commander unwillingly ordered the attack to begin.

Meanwhile back at Terror's main base. Sergeant Bash and the other captive marines had made their escape taking with them others that were prisoners. A lone guard watched them disappear before he was burnt to death by a flamethrower. Another guard turned and ran to make his report to Terror. Terror was listening to the complaints his people were complaining about.

"You said that no one could defeat us. And yet Magic Force is defeating us" a drone resident said to Terror.

Terror knocked the unfortunate drone down "Listen fool! I give the orders! This is war! Evil loses battles but in the end evil will win that I promise all of you. Now Greendeath and Destructor will capture the leader's friend and bring her to me. I will kill that friend and then when Kimberly comes into the castle looking for her kidnapped friend, I'll kill her and take the Magicsaber of Light!" Terror said.

"Mighty One the prisoners escaped!" the lone guard said.

Immediately Railbuster seized him "You! A worthless guard! Tell us that you're lying or Terror will rip you to bits!"

"Please, I was with the other guard before he was burnt to destruction" the guard said.

Now it was Terror's turn to grip the guard "You were supposed to be watching over them!"

"I was mighty one," the drone croaked out before Terror's claws destroyed him in front of the frightened crowd.

"This is whats going to happen to you all if you fail my plan" Terror said.

The crowd snapped into obedience.

"Nice plan um when will this victory come in?"

"Soon my people soon" Terror said to the unfortunate drone that spoke out.

Railbuster looked at Terror. "What is it Railbuster?"

"Should I send out our troops to catch the marines?"

Terror thought about the question before answering "No, those marines are nothing for Kimberly to get upset over if we catch and kill them. Oh by killing her brother made her mad but killing her friend is going to make her madder" Terror said.

"Right so let them get away?"

"Yes, we have no need for them" Terror said walking to his chamber with his sidekick.

Meanwhile on the battlefield, things were getting intense. Jack Lateint the Nutralisk Leader and his companion, Snipper were snipping Terror's Forces left and right but no matter what they done more and more kept on coming.

"They are more on the offensive rather than defending themselves," Kimberly said.

"Why?" Moonshine asked herself.

Flower fired many rounds herself but she had to go to other places to fire as she fired ten rounds avoiding electric blasts as she ran. Other Magic Troopers were just like her but few were unlucky and fell slain. Magic Cavilers ran out to engage the enemy giving most of the Magic Troopers more time.

Kimberly nodded to Moonshine it was time to call upon the myth units. Once more the mighty Dragons, Hydra, and Medusa were called out. This time the tide of Battle changed immediately when the Myth units came out roaring their way through the battle field by spewing fire, biting or clawing, shooting or freezing every enemy that was too slow.

"The myth units are out Commanders you want us to retreat?" a drone solider asked.

Greendeath put the drone's answer down roughly "Not until we get the leaders friend!"

"Triangleships begin bombing run!" Kimberly and Moonshine ordered.

Triangleships filled the air right then bombing the unsuspected drones below. Kimberly's Magicsaber sent out two more beams. Two more units came out of it one was a circular triangular ship with two magic laser cannons. The circular part of the ship was attached to the triangular body of the fighter.

"Magic Fighter Magic Force's main fighter jet" Moonshine said.

The Magic Fighters flew out into the action they were joined up with ships that looked like oak tree leaves stuck together.

"Nutralisk Leaf Fighters" Snipper said.

"Looks like I have a lot to learn about Nutralisk" Lightspirit said taking out a row of advancing Assassin Drones with his Destructive Flame God Power.

Out of the last beam Kimberly's Magicsaber of Light sent out came out a powerful dangerous looking fighter jet of all. It was a dangerous black fighter jet looking ship. On each wing was four magic laser cannons. It had eight all together. In the front part of the fighter was a dangerous looking beam device. Kimberly could tell the middle also had something dangerous. The sight of this fighter was so great that it scared General Moonshine and General Goldsupervena but the Battlebot General recovered quickly and continued to fight the opposing army waving his Magicsaber expertly.

"What is it Moonshine?" Kimberly asked.

"The most powerful unit of all, the Black Thunder!" Moonshine said.

"I thought the Magicsaber of Light is the strongest unit," Kimberly admitted as her Magicsaber sliced threw a Nuclear Drone.

Moonshine shook her head and blasted an Assassin Drone that was about to sneak up on a fallen Magic Trooper to finish him off "That's weapon not unit Kimberly, anyway the Black Thunder has not only eight Magic lasers, but a charge laser beam, powerful shields that can not be warn off. The same type of shields as Magic Fighters have

Magic Shields which wear off any type of attack, then Reflector and even Back off shields, it also has a Killer Device which is why it's the most powerful unit ever."

"Um, what's the Killer exactly supposed to be?" Kimberly asked, as she got ready to destroy another drone.

"A powerful Magic Attack that wipes out every thing in one blow it is the same power as a normal Magicsaber, not even buildings are safe. I have the same ability to do so but am afraid to use it since it can kill good as well" Moonshine said as she and Kimberly to an electric Drone down.

Suddenly while Flower was firing away an Electric Drone snuck up behind the overwhelmed girl. Somehow it knew she was the leader's best friend and raised it's hand. Sixth since moved into Flower right away she turned and fired her Magic Snipping Rifle just as the Electric Drone fired it's electrical blast it was both sent for stun and kill. Both hit each other, Flower screamed as the Electric Drone's electricity hit and stunned her. But the Electric Drone was fatally damaged and malfunctioning but was able to grab Flower and toss her over his head and walk towards Greendeath and Destructor. It was able to give out it's last speech as it gave the now completely stunned Flower to the Commanders "Here's the leader's friend" before exploding.

"Looks like we got what we wanted" Greendeath said throwing the stunned girl over his shoulder. Destructor just turned with sorrow trying to ignore Greendeath's comment, right then Flower knew something was different about this Assassin Drone.

Kimberly made an attempt to rescue her friend and charged wielding the Magicsaber of Light slicing drones to size as their commanders singled a retreat. Fifty drones stood waiting for her giving their commanders time to escape. The drones launched themselves on the charging girl regardless of their safety. Kimberly was buried in no time as she went down.

Moonshine looked at General Goldsupervena whom was running to help Kimberly but she held him back.

"She'll get killed" the Battlebot General said.

"No, charging them would only make it worse. There's one choice to get her free unharmed. Though I've never thought I need to use it." Goldsupervena stopped his charge as Lightspirit asked, "What do you have in mind? General Goldsupervena what does she mean?"

Goldsupervena knew it was pointless to argue with Moonshine so he decided to speak for both creatures "Moonshine is going to use the Killer ability of hers. It's very dangerous though I've never seen it. It'll kill all drones but also our troops as well."

"That's much too dangerous Moonshine not only will you destroy the overwhelming drones on Kimberly but Kimberly herself" Lightspirit pointed out after the words sunk into him.

"No, Lightspirit it won't kill her, isn't there a defense God Power that can protect us all from the blast?"

"Yes" Lightspirit said blankly.

"I must admit myself that its risky but if your willing to help we might be able to save her from the Killer blast are you willing to try?" Moonshine asked a bit sad of her own decision of using the Killer.

"If you are willing to do your part, so what do you want Lightspirit to do?" Lightspirit said sounding really excited and disappointed at the same time.

"Now we have to do it just right, Lightspirit you will have to summon that defending God Power. While I gather the magical energy. When I fire that's when Lightspirit will summon it. Everyone stay out of the area if you want to live the rest of your life" Moonshine ordered.

"Okay summon it when you fire" Lightspirit said getting ready to summon the God power.

Moonshine stood on her two hooves like a human; spread her front hooves wide open and closed her eyes to concentrate on getting the energy from the area. A small dangerous whitish looking ball appeared over her head. The ball quickly grew larger and larger as more energy was placed into the ball until it was as big as a baseball.

"On the count of three send it down Lightspirit. Now to everyone stand where I am in order to avoid the blast!" Moonshine said.

"Okay" Lightspirit said spreading his paws wide.

"One..." Moonshine began as the ball grew.

"Two..." Goldsupervena said.

"Three **KILLER BLAST!**" Moonshine said releasing the ball.

"Heavens Shield!" Lightspirit said.

A shield made of pure yellow light came down and went threw the piled up drones that were on Kimberly and went above her. Kimberly could only see the yellow shielding light and then saw a big white ball coming straight towards her. Immediately she knew what it was.

"Oh-no, General Moonshine used the Killer! I'm going to die" Kimberly said to herself.

She closed her eyes as the ball hit. To everyone keeping away from the blast, they saw a white explosion. The explosion was huge sending tons of magical energy among the enemy drones. Unfortunately the swirling winds from the blast was too much for the thousands of Magic Troopers, and Nutralisk alike, they flew backwards into the trees and they were alive but shaken

Kimberly closed her eyes and waited for death to come to her then suddenly everything was silent. She opened her eyes and saw that every drone on her was destroyed and then that the Killer blast vanished cracking the protecting light shield and destroyed it. Kimberly struggled pushing the fifty drones off of her. Moonshine noticed Kent ridding Swift to help Kimberly up.

"Wait Kent the side effects of Magic could be down there!" the unicorn warned.

Kent ignored her warning he was worried more about Kimberly's life not his.

Professor Strike smiled at Moonshine "He's my boy, he gets those ideas from me."

"Well he's you son but please tell him not to ignore orders please"

"Um, Moonshine you're the General of Magic Force's air and

Myth Unit command. It's logical that Kent wouldn't listen to you" Lightspirit pointed out.

"True, um Goldsupervena you're the sensible one, could you talk to him for me?" Moonshine asked.

"Of course Moonshine, us Generals after all need to work together to keep Magic Force standing" General Goldsupervena said.

"Thanks let's get down there" Moonshine said detecting it was safe to go down there.

Kent reached Kimberly and helped her up patting her to make sure she was not hurt "Kimberly I was worried about you. I thought I'd lose you in that fight. You aren't hurt are you?"

Kimberly shook her head "I'm fine Kent. I appreciate you caring for me. But they took my friend Flower! I must go after them," Kimberly said.

Moonshine and Goldsupervena came down. They heard Kimberly's tone.

"Relax Kimberly" Moonshine advised here.

"Yes, evil will use your anger to their advantage" Goldsupervena said recalling the time Railbuster trapped him in a small room and dueled him trying to defeat him by using his brother's anger against him. He almost succeeded but Goldsupervena won in the end because of Moonshine's sharp notice that he went missing for a few hours.

"Besides you need a plan Lady Kimberly, my sensors tell me that she is going to be taken to Terror, this is what the Gods have been fearing today, Flower's capture" Lightspirit began then he noticed that everyone was starring at him then added on "The cause is still unknown."

"Give us you best guess Lightspirit" Professor Strike said to him.

"Well, I'm guessing that the Gods are watching over Magic Force"

"That would make since if they sent a message to you that stated something wasn't right" Kimberly said.

"General Goldsupervena how defended is the military base?" Kimberly said.

"Very defended, Terror will use everything against you and if you go in the castle it may turn out to be a trap," Goldsupervena said.

"I agree, the evil Assassin Drone's forces are at full power there," a voice sounded.

Kimberly, the remaining members of Magic Force and the Nutralisk Force turned to see a tough marine.

"Sergeant Bash, Tommy's best friend" Goldsupervena said.

"I hear two of our special agents are generals," the marine said looking at Goldsupervena and Moonshine.

"Yes we are" Moonshine said proudly.

To prove he was a serious general Goldsupervena tapped Kent lightly on the head.

"What is it General?" Kent asked.

"Kent, I know you love Kimberly, but do not ignore another generals commands even if she isn't the commanding general. She is experienced in Magic and whatever she says will go along with me. Please don't let me go over this lecture again Commander" Goldsupervena said.

Kent looked embarrassed for the first time "Okay, General"

General Moonshine looked at her friend; Goldsupervena puzzled this lecture was how the Battlebot was going to speak to ones that didn't obey her. She swore under her breath that if Kent were in her command she would've given him a serious lecture.

Goldsupervena looked at her "You said it yourself Moonshine, that he's in love with Lady Kimberly, so that's why I let it slide" He turned to Kent and grew serious "The next time you disobey Moonshine and it isn't for the fact that you love Kimberly you will be having a stern lecture. So don't let me hear that you did so Commander."

"I promise not to General Goldsupervena. Sorry for disobeying you Moonshine"

"It's okay I forgive you"

"Goldsupervena you sounded just like Captain Tommy when you gave Kent that part of the lecture. I remember that's what he said to people that loved each other" Sergeant Bash pointed out.

Kimberly shook out of laughter at the mention of her brother's name and rank then ask the marine the question she dreaded the most, "Did my brother die fighting or a coward?" she asked.

"Your brother as I knew him and saw him went down fighting to the very last moment of his life. And by a deadly trick, Terror stabbed him with the Magicsaber of Darkness in the chest and it was all over within seconds he didn't even get the chance to utter his dying words" the marine said.

Kimberly's eyes filled with tears as she uttered out happily "That does sound like my brother fighting to the last moment. He said to me once: if I have to die, I rather make it a quick death taking my enemies with me"

"And he did just that though we also lost Lady Sea in the process of trying to revolt against him" Sergeant Bash said looking at Jack Lateint.

"I'm sorry, I was aiming for Terror and she got in the way of my arrow" Jack said.

"Apology accepted" Bash said.

"Bash join forces with Magic Force and I swear I'll bring Terror down to his knees!" Kimberly said.

"That's a brave girl but General Goldsupervena is right, all allied forces will lose a lot of men" Sergeant Bash said.

Moonshine looked at Kimberly, "Not exactly Sergeant, with the Black Thunder Kimberly we could actually win the last battle against Terror"

Kimberly smiled "Right I have a plan"

"Tell us Lady Kimberly" Goldsupervena said.

"Moonshine, for once you will be given full command of Magic Force, Goldsupervena and I will go inside the castle with about one thousand Magic Troopers to rescue Flower. But before that it is up to you and the other members of the Nutralisk Forces and whats left of the USA's military to distract them" Kimberly said.

"Okay sounds easy for us but how do you plan to go inside the castle without Terror knowing about you?" Sergeant Bash asked.

"I'll take the Black Thunder in with it's speed as Moonshine predicts, we shall go inside the ship and come back out unharmed if all goes well. What do you think of that Goldsupervena?" Kimberly said.

The Battlebot didn't need any second bidding for a rescue attempt as long as he was with his mistress at all times he liked whatever he was hearing "That's a great idea Lady Kimberly!" the Battlebot said.

Moonshine groaned "I think you didn't get the picture that time but I'll do the diversion" Moonshine said shaking her head.

Chapter 15
The Final Duels

Greendeath and Destructor carried the now recovering Flower on their backs. She groaned a bit and sat up straight. Greendeath noticed her recovering, but didn't make a move to threaten his captive. Flower right then noticed what he was thinking of.

"Put me down drone or I'll make soup out of you" Flower threatened.

The threat stunned Greendeath but he returned his own comment when he saw Destructor turn and laugh at his companion's face reaction to the threat "Mighty Terror will slay you girl! If Terror wouldn't have ordered the capture of you, you would've died by my radiation!"

Destructor kept on laughing "He, he, that's really funny, turning him into soup that'll be the day."

Flower was forced to giggle herself when Destructor put it that way.

"Hey you put me down, and I'll let Kimberly spare you, Destructor" Flower begged the Assassin Drone.

"Sorry I'd love to free you, you silly girl but I've got to listen to

Terror the Assassin. Listen I didn't want to capture you " Destructor said felling sorry for his victim.

"I guess it's hard being a drone listening to Terror" Flower said trying to bait the Assassin Drone.

"You bet, fail him and he kills you" Destructor said sadly and easily baited.

Greendeath wasn't affected by the speeches Flower was saying, "Destructor! Don't let her convince you of letting her go. Listen girl, save your talking for later!"

Flower knew it was hopeless to get free so she became quite as the two carried her along. The sight of Terror's castle scared Flower half to death. Not only did the sight scare her but the feeling it had. She never felt an evil feeling so great before in her life. Terror's commanders carried her to Terror. Terror turned to his commanders.

"Ah part one victory complete you may put her down now but please make sure she doesn't escape" Terror said.

Flower gulped but tried to sound brave as she shouted; "Holding me captive won't help you!"

Terror looked at Flower "Oh, it will you see I don't plan to keep you living."

Suddenly Flower heard something open and then the dangerous hiss of the Magicsaber of Darkness. She then knew what Terror meant, "Then kill me! Kimberly will not settle for this she hasn't forgave you from…" Flower began but she would never finish the sentence as Terror ran up to her throat, ripped out her throat, and stabbed her right threw her stomach. Both the ripping of her neck and the Magicsaber of Darkness did their work, Flower died instantly. Terror looked at Flower's still form and kicked her corpse.

"Take this body away and place it in the open where Kimberly can find her" Terror commanded his commanders.

They saluted him and done his commands and disappeared.

Terror looked at Railbuster as Magic Force, Nutralisk Forces, and USA Forces pummeled his own military units.

"It's time. You know what to do" Terror told him.

Railbuster nodded "Finally time to get my revenge I've always wanted. You eight stay here with Terror others please be at every turn. I don't want you to kill my brother, I must fight him alone" Railbuster said vanishing.

Meanwhile outside Magic Force and it's allies were fighting against Terror's forces for the final time. General Moonshine knew it was for the last time, as she addressed to her troops, and allies "Friends, this is the last battle. This will determined the fate of the world. Remember this if you die, you die fighting for Freedom, Life, liberty, and the pursuit of happiness! All or most enemies must be destroyed! Now our distraction is working I see that Black Thunder going into the castle.

"Becareful Kimberly" Kent said through his headset.

"I will Kent" Kimberly called down.

Kimberly landed the Black Thunder down while her friends and allies fought the enemy forces. Once inside they were greeted by Terror's men, which they were no match to Kimberly or General Goldsupervena's troops. When they reached the middle area, they heard the doors lock.

"It's a trap!" the Battlebot general said.

"Okay you were once here right?" Kimberly said.

"That's right Lady Kimberly" Goldsupervena said as he and his troops surrounded the leader of Magic Force.

Kimberly took charge of the situation immediately "Then go try and resolve the trap, take half of our men."

"What about you?" Goldsupervena asked already not liking the idea of separation.

"With my half, I'll go find Flower and save her before something awful happens to her" Kimberly said.

The Battlebot nodded his head thoughtfully "Okay Lady Kimberly, but please be safe."

Kimberly nodded her head and replied, "I will General."

With two last nods the two separated. It was harder for Kimberly to find the direction of the base than to Goldsupervena. She knew that she should've known the direction of the base; her brother took her there almost every time he was off work.

"Ahhh...You made it this far with no problem. Well too bad you will die eventually." A random voice said.

Kimberly and her five hundred Magic Troopers entered one room and looked around. Kimberly found a girl's body and rushed to the body. She then felt the body and then knew it was Flower.

"Flower your..." Kimberly began she was going to say alive but then she noticed her friend's neck and the stab wound from a Magicsaber.

"Dead" she finished in betweens sobs.

"That's right and I'm proud of killing her," a mechanical voice sounded.

Kimberly turned to see a huge Assassin Drone standing his ground what she didn't make out was that eight Electric Drones were standing invisible. The drones were told that if the battle was going against Terror to shot his foe down.

Kimberly turned to her Magic Troopers "Go leave Terror to me" then she turned to Terror the Assassin and tried to sound tough towards the Assassin Drone, "Terror why her? Now I can understand my brother but why her she didn't do anything to you"

"Ah, I knew you'd get angry at me for doing so that's why I did it plus she destroyed precious men of mine" Terror said trying to use Kimberly's anger against her.

"That won't work Terror, when I found out that you killed my brother I made a vow to destroy you. Plus now killing my best friend I shall have two vows to destroy you. I must do so but I will defeat you Terror without a negative thought so you can not use it against me" Kimberly said. She sent herself at him with a stab, he dodged but she hit two drones.

"Strong words girl but for any reason, I'll destroy you and I'll take the Magicsaber of Light as my reward" Terror said as he enlightened the Magicsaber of Darkness. Immediately Kimberly's Magicsaber of Light came into play! Terror made the first move as the two foes circled one another.

The two Magicsabers of ether Light and Darkness clashed violently protecting their owners from harm. Kimberly knew that Terror was also an Assassin Drone and that his mechanical legs and arms could do a lot of damage to her if he succeeded by ripping her own throat out. Kimberly suddenly knew Terror had an Advantage. His blade was nowhere to be seen but her Magicsaber of Light was visible. As the Assassin Drone's blade clashed against the Magicsaber of Light, Kimberly recalled the time her brother taught her that sight can be deceiving at times, it was better to listen to the sounds of the item your foe was wielding.

"Here, We shall do battle in the future were everything will be dark and destroyed when I am done."

A loud clash erupted bringing Kimberly out of her trance. The scene around Kimberly changed to a world where all buildings had marks of fires and tornados. More buildings were damaged more than others. Kimberly looked around and saw a dead person who reminded her of her brother.

"You care too much about your brother" Terror's voice sounded.

Kimberly shrugged off the comment easily "At least Tommy and I cared for each other! You drones could hardly care for one another. You're just a big pile of scrap metal. You were truly recycled by the humans"

Terror got angry at the insult and struck violently legs and Magicsaber of Darkness together. Kimberly dodged the Magicsaber swipe but the Assassin Drone's legs barely found it's mark. They ranked Kimberly exposing her spine.

"Ouch!" Kimberly said.

"Oh, that's right you female humans take injuries seriously" Terror said watching Kimberly trying to recover from the attack placing an arm on her injured back.

Kimberly looked at him "At least I can do more than that!" She raised her blade and the Magicsaber of Light shot out a blast of pure magical white light. The blast sent the Assassin sprawling against the wall harmed.

Both Terror and ignored their wounds and continued to attack one another. Terror jumped onto a building ledge. Kimberly jumped up to but Terror grabbed her shirt and threw her higher than him.

Meanwhile some sixth since warned General Goldsupervena that Kimberly was in danger. But he was ordered to find the release switch to turn off the red alert. This machine released all closed doors. He knew there were four of them but finding two was just enough for an escape. The Battlebot General found one and dialed the emergency lock code and sent if for it to disable two of the machines. Upon doing so his forces collided with Terror's Forces. He made his way back with only twenty men left. Suddenly out of nowhere a beam of red light came out and hit the nearest Magic Trooper killing him instantly. Then more and more beams came out. General Goldsupervena ordered his troops to go on the ground and crawl their way to where the Black Thunder lay. The ones that were too slow found themselves killed by a mysterious red beam. Only ten remained by the time the attacks ended and most were making their way to the Black Thunder when Railbuster stepped out his Magicsaber enlightened.

"Why if it isn't my brother, or should I say General Goldsupervena" Railbuster said.

Goldsupervena looked at his brother "So then my brother, it is time"

"Indeed I've been waiting for this" Railbuster said as he walked towards his brother.

General Goldsupervena drew his Magicsaber "I hoped this would never happen Railbuster but it has to end like this."

"Yes, who will win this last fight between us, my good brother Goldsupervena or Terror's second in command me Railbuster?" Railbuster said.

"Let's find out," Goldsupervena said as the two Battlebots clashed their blades together.

"Go Magic Troopers, you will all be safe in the Black Thunder go inside it, I have a score to settle once and for all" Goldsupervena said as his Magicsaber clashed onto Railbuster's for the second time.

"But general?" a Magic Trooper began.

"Do you know how to carry out an order? This is a personal issue now go!" Goldsupervena said.

"Yes, General" the Magic Trooper said as he jumped into the Black Thunder. The two Battlebots clashed blades once more. Then the battle between the two Battlebots began clashing everywhere violently. Somehow Goldsupervena saw a big purple thing in the air. It was a huge circular thing. He kicked Railbuster in the chest making him fly backwards.

"Still? You still get hit by the move. How sad." Goldsupervena jumped up to the circular thing. He noticed it was bigger then the building. He also noticed Railbuster coming at him with a stab.

"You wish you could use the same moves on me but I am learning." Railbuster said flying at Goldsupervena. Goldsupervena jumped up into the air and came back down on Railbuster.

"Nope. You still do the same moves and I hit you with the same moves"

Meanwhile Moonshine and the rest of Magic Force were actually doing quite well. They were succeeding in pushing the enemies back towards their fortress. Moonshine's magical sensing abilities told her Kimberly and even Goldsupervena were in trouble of losing their lives. To Moonshine's eyes she saw the Magicsaber of Light clashing against the darkness.

"The clash of the two powerful Magicsabers are beginning, only one will still stand" Moonshine said.

Lightspirit looked up at the sky "That's exactly what the Gods were meaning. They knew this was going to happen who will fall? No one knows."

Dragons, Hydra, and Medusa gave Magic Force the key advantage over many enemies.

Clash! Hiss, the Magicsabers of Light and Darkness clashed violently many times. Kimberly was young an energetic but Terror was quicker and a much more agile in dodging attacks. Terror knocked Kimberly onto the ground with a headbut to the chest. Kimberly collapsed trying to catch her breath as Terror ran at her. Kimberly waited for the last possible moment and dodged as the Assassin Drone leapt up at her. Terror flew past her his arms swung the Magicsaber of Darkness as he passed her. Kimberly blocked it with the Magicsaber of Light and kicked Terror. Terror went flying overhead landing on the ground hard. Kimberly ran over to Terror but the spider was quick and leapt onto a higher ground. Kimberly watched Terror. Terror raised his Magicsaber of Darkness and fired a beam at Kimberly. Kimberly barely dodged the blast as she jumped up to engage Terror. As soon as she landed he fired another beam once more. Kimberly this time was struck by the blast. She closed her eyes as darkness tried to consume her. Terror ran at her again and this time grabbed her right leg and ripped it to the bone. Kimberly looked at her leg.

Terror grinned wickedly, "Your near death Lady Kimberly" Terror said as she jumped away. He grabbed her by her stomach and lifted her up in one claw then in the other claw he picked up the Magicsaber of Darkness to spear her through. Kimberly kicked out with her left leg and kicked Terror's Magicsaber of Darkness onto the ground below. Terror looked at her "Even if I don't have the Magicsaber of Darkness with me, I can still kill you."

Terror threw Kimberly off of the platform she was on.

"AHH, No!" Kimberly shouted as she fell then added on "I've failed you Tommy."

Kimberly landed on Flower's body. Kimberly was relieved that she landed on something soft. She watched as Terror jumped off the board. She knew exactly what he was after, so she gathered up the Magical energy in the Magicsaber of Light and fired it at Terror. The blast hit him in the eye blinding the Assassin Drone for a few seconds.

This was all Kimberly needed for she grabbed the Magicsaber of Darkness. The saber's hilt sent a jolt of electricity into her hand then into her entire body, she knew right then that it was trying to corrupt her with it's evil powers. At the same time, her own true Magicsaber of Light sent the same shock into her trying to stop all of the evil powers that were flowing through her. Kimberly couldn't take the shocks from both Magicsabers she threw the Magicsaber of Darkness away from herself and into a trashcan. Terror recovered from Kimberly's Magicsaber blast and saw her standing there trying to recover and looking at the Magicsaber of Light wondering what overcame it to shock her. Terror charged at her. Kimberly recovered and watched as Terror ran towards her. Terror leapt at her legs flailing. With the last of her strength Kimberly raised her blade and swung. She was rewarded with a shock of despair as the Magicsaber of Light cut threw Terror's body. She watched as it cut him in half. The upper half of him missed her by inches but his lower half succeeded in hitting her arm ripping it out of it's socket. Kimberly watched Terror's body hit the ground sliced in half never to rise again. With the remaining arm in place she made her way to Flower and collapsed waiting as she spoke out "I did it, I lived long enough to revenge you my brother and good friend Flower." Then she became unconscious waiting for death to overtake her.

Goldsupervena was having the fight of his life. Railbuster was indeed stronger than he last met him. No matter the cause the Battlebot thought, he must be stopped. The duel continued and Goldsupervena lead his brother outside where battle raged.

"Holly cow looks like Goldsupervena and Railbuster are at it again!" Sergeant Bash mumbled.

"This time it looks like it's to the finish this time" Moonshine said.

"Get em general, show him that you are superior win this one" Lightspirit said gladly but deep inside he knew Kimberly was in trouble. His feelings reached Moonshine whom noticed him.

"Something wrong?" she asked.

"Yes, General Moonshine, Kimberly's in danger!" Lightspirit said.

"General Goldsupervena! Did you resolve the doors?" Moonshine asked.

Goldsupervena heard the shout and blocked Railbuster's Magicsaber "Yes, general"

"Good then were going in to save Kimberly, just keep on fighting your brother" Moonshine said.

"Well do" Goldsupervena said as his blade clashed against Railbuster's.

Moonshine led her force and allied forces into the fortress while the two gigantic Battlebots fought on. Lighting began to flash as the Battlebots fought on and suddenly rain started to fall on the battlefield. They fought all the way to a bell tower. Railbuster had trapped his brother against the bell tower of the castle.

"I have you now" Railbuster sneered.

"You forgot, I have the brains to pull this one off," Goldsupervena said as he leapt over his brother and kicked him near the bell tower giving him an extra boast.

Railbuster got up and found himself trapped near the bell tower.

"You planned this all along!" Railbuster shouted.

"Yes, I did" Goldsupervena said.

Railbuster sliced out at his brother but his brother cleverly blocked the blade in his.

"You are strong brother good's strength flows through you well," Railbuster said.

"Yes" Goldsupervena said as he took a kick to his chest. He then clapped his fist together and sent out a magic beam. The beam hit Railbuster in the chest creating another hole in him.

"What?! Not again!" Railbuster said to himself looking at his brand new hole.

"Give up?" Goldsupervena asked.

"Why should I? This is to the death plus after one lucky move I don't think so" Railbuster said.

Goldsupervena looked at him "I really don't want to destroy you but you make me to do so" the Battlebot general clapped his fist together and sent out another beam out of both his fist and his Magicsaber. Fearing that the magic beam his brother sent at him from his fist was the most damaging attack, Railbuster blocked the huge magic beam blast and sent it onto the ground below but Goldsupervena's Magicsaber beam cut his left hand off. Railbuster roared out he was losing once again and this time the better Battlebot was Goldsupervena. Railbuster finally looked into Goldsupervena's eyes. He finally understood his brother's feeling, his brother was only defeating him for the purpose of good. Railbuster knew that he was powerless to fight back now unless he could use Goldsupervena's feelings of peace and protection to his advantage.

He tried a last desperate speech movement before coming up with a plan.

"Brother, you win…I can never defeat you…I take back what I said to you earlier, I will let you go"

Goldsupervena stopped and considered the fact "A wise choice my brother now if you excuse me I must go to the aide of my mistress."

The Battlebot turned and started to walk towards the castle. Railbuster grinned his brother fell for the trick he made a desperate attack and charged his Magicsaber in a spear position. He charged ready to spear Goldsupervena through. He would've succeeded if it wasn't for the fact for his feet, which sounded like thunder on the ramparts. Goldsupervena stopped as he heard the charge he spun around, neatly avoided the Magicsaber attack and his Magicsaber cut through Railbuster horizontally through the middle. Goldsupervena watched as Railbuster's body fell to the ground never to get up and fight again.

"How'd he do that?" Railbuster asked as his eyes closed in death.

"You'll never find out now," Goldsupervena said as he withdrew his Magicsaber and made his way to his mistress. On his way down he met Moonshine and her group.

"I take it you won by the look on your face" Moonshine said.
Goldsupervena nodded "I did. Now we must find Kimberly. Lightspirit is she living?"

"She's alive but barely," Lightspirit answered. Magic Force, Nutralisk Force, and the USA soldiers ran to a door. The door opened and in it laid Kimberly's still form.

"Kimberly!" Kent shouted as he ran into the room.

Immediately electricity sounded and General Goldsupervena jumped into Kent's way took the damage for him.

"General Goldsupervena!" Moonshine said to him as Goldsupervena fell heavily damaged by the eight electrical blasts.

"Its nothing," the Battlebot general said getting up.

Once more the Electric Drones fired again, this time Lightspirit took them advantage over the situation.

"Lighting Field!" Lightspirit shouted pointing to where he saw the electrical blast coming from.

Moonshine called upon the magical powers and designated the beams. The sky around the Electric Drones filled with lighting and fell from the sky like mad hornets. Horrifying explosions sounded right then giving Magic Force and its allies the information that the drones were destroyed.

Lightspirit turned to Goldsupervena.

"I'm alright," Goldsupervena said.

"Will you survive?" Lightspirit asked spreading his paws wide.

"Yes, Moonshine has already used a magical power that takes away the damage marks, I'll recover, we Battlebots if we stayed loyal to the good side have the ability to heal over a short period of time" Goldsupervena said proudly.

"Thanks General I didn't think that the drones would've been here, maybe Kimberly was killed by them" Kent said.

Lightspirit looked at Kimberly's ruined body then shook his head sadly "No, the markings on her body indicate that she wasn't killed by those Electric Drones."

"Then what harmed her?" Kent asked not fully understanding Lightspirit's comment.

Moonshine whispered "Light on" and her horn glue with the same colored light as the Magicsaber of Light, lighted up the room.

"Why couldn't you've done that sooner or later we would've seen the drones then" Kent complained.

"Don't complain to a General, Commander" General Goldsupervena said.

"I.I.I. Sorry General Moonshine" Kent said.

"It's okay, I understand how you feel, now I see what done this" the unicorn general said.

General Goldsupervena bent over his mistress.

"Assassin Drone work alright"

Jack found the upper half of Terror while Professor Strike saw the lower half of Terror.

"Looks like Terror and Kimberly fought each other to the death" Moonshine said looking at Terror.

"Sea would've wanted to help her if she were alive" Sergeant Bash said.

"She would've too Bash" a marine said to him.

Lightspirit knelt down to Kimberly, then saw what could've been the cause and for the first time froze.

"Lightspirit is there a freeze drone in here?" Jack Lateint asked the Battlebot.

"No, it's just that, I found Flower's body only she's not living, this could've been the cause of the fighting. Kimberly saw Flower dead and saw Terror standing alive," Lightspirit said.

"Well, is Kimberly alive?" Kent asked looking at her right leg and completely ripped out arm.

"These wounds would've killed a lesser human but she is alive but barely. I'll need to act fast and so do the Gods if I am to save her life and bring Flower back to life" Lightspirit said looking at his friends.

All of Lightspirit's friends nodded their heads in agreement for everyone loved Kimberly. Goldsupervena had two thoughts the fact that he would've broke Kimberly's mother's promise that he'd protect her all the way. And the other was what would happen to the Magicsaber of Light? Would it ever come on again? Lightspirit nodded back.

"Let's hope that it's not too late to heal Kimberly and Flower. **HEAVEN'S HEAL!**" the magic wielding Battlebot spread his paws wide and unleashed the powerful yellow lights of heaven.

The yellow light hit both Kimberly and Flower. It regrew Flower's throat skin and all, plus brought her to life once more. For Kimberly, it put her arm back to normal; rehealed her wounded leg and back skin.

Kimberly opened her eyes wide "I thought I was a goner" she said.

Kent scooped her up "Kimberly your safe" he said kissing her.

Kimberly smiled at him as she kissed back "I won for Flower and for my brother, Terror lies dead."

"Terror! That little Assassin Drone he ripped my throat out!" Flower shouted in anger.

"Flower? Your alive?" Kimberly asked.

Flower turned to Kimberly and felt her own neck "My neck it's not ripped out."

"That did kill you, the Gods have brought you back to life Commander. Know that they can only do this two more times" Lightspirit said interrupting the two reunited girls.

"I was dead?" Flower asked.

Kimberly nodded "You were Flower. After your capture I followed you and I tried to rescue you right then but was buried by Terror's Drones. Once I got here, Goldsupervena and I made our way into this place. Turned out it was a trap so I had to send your commanding general on a mission to allow us to get out of the castle safely looks like none of the Magic Troopers in his group survived" Kimberly said.

Goldsupervena thought about this before interrupting his mistress politely "Lady Kimberly, sorry for the interruption but during the mission you sent me on, I had many run-ins with the enemy force plus by the time I accomplished my mission and was coming back to help you out Railbuster stepped out and engaged me but before doing so took out ten out of the twenty Magic Troopers that remained alive."

"Okay so I know where the other five hundred went but where did you put the remaining ten troops?" Kimberly asked looking confused.

"In the Black Thunder, Lady Kimberly I told them to go in it while I was dueling Railbuster."

"Okay, so I take it that you won the duel" Flower said as Kimberly turned to her friend.

"Yes, I did but got heavily wounded and became unconscious losing blood fast" Kimberly said.

Lightspirit took a good pause himself before answering his leader "Lady Kimberly, your wounds were fatal and you could've died from blood loss, if the Gods haven't been watching you then you would've died leaving Kent behind."

Kimberly understood but then saw Goldsupervena stumble.

"General Goldsupervena! Are you okay?" Kimberly asked as she ran over to him.

"For the most part but I've been wounded trying to protect Kent" the Battlebot general said.

"Kent did you hurt him?" Kimberly asked.

"No, he didn't Kimberly. We didn't see those Electric Drones waiting for us to come in. Once my son saw you lying on the ground he thought you were dead and rushed over to help save you if you were living. But he was shot at by those Electric Drones" Professor Strike said.

"Oh, sorry for the accusing then" Kimberly said apologizing to Kent.

"You had the right to accuse me," Kent said.

"So Goldsupervena saw the blasts coming right towards you and stepped in front of them taking the blows for you" Flower said.

"Yes, and I'd do the same for you Commander Flower"

Goldsupervena said taking his Magicsaber out and saluting with it. Kimberly took one last look around the castle.

"One more thing before we leave, um Goldsupervena don't reach into the trash can" Kimberly said suddenly remembering what she'd done to the Magicsaber of Darkness.

Goldsupervena took one step closer to the trashcan and looked into it. He saw the Magicsaber of Darkness glowing rapidly.

"Holly cow! Lady Kimberly you didn't touch the Magicsaber of Darkness did you?" Goldsupervena asked.

"I did trying to block Terror from using it against me and I have a question for you and maybe Professor Strike could answer this as well" Kimberly said as she stayed near Kent not moving to the trashcan as if she feared the blade.

"Anything Lady Kimberly. I'll try to answer it to the best of my abilities" the Battlebot General said.

"I will try to help as well," Moonshine said.

"Okay ask away," Professor Strike said.

Kimberly looked at everyone before answering, "This is about the Magicsaber of Darkness. Um, when I grabbed the Magicsaber of Darkness's handle to throw it away it sent a shock through my body as if trying to corrupt me with it's evil. But at the same time I held the Magicsaber of Light which sent the same shock through me trying to get rid of the evil…my question is, what was going on?"

Goldsupervena looked around "Does not compute."

Moonshine looked confused as well "All I know is that whoever grips the Magicsaber of Darkness's handle gets a shock which corrupts them overtime. I don't have a clue what happened" Moonshine said.

Professor Strike knelt down to Kimberly and asked the question that would confirm his answer for her.

"Kimberly, let me ask you this. What did it feel like the Magicsabers of Light and Darkness were doing when they shocked you?"

"Well it felt like one was over powering another in the beginning but then were going to become equal in me" Kimberly said.

"That is something dreadful. It confirms the prophecy of the two Magicsabers uniting. The person who grips the Magicsaber of Darkness becomes engulfed in evil forever. However if one and the only one grips the Magicsaber of Light he or in your case she has become engulfed in the good side forever. However if the two Magicsabers unite both will try to overcome the other at first but then together cancel each other out resulting in death or a person half-evil-half good all of their lives" Professor Strike said.

"Oh-my-gosh! I could've died if I didn't throw it into the trash can" Kimberly said.

"Yes, it could've but you did an excellent job of throwing it away before they killed you" Kent said.

"Now the only thing is somehow we must destroy the Magicsaber of Darkness but we must do it in front of the people of the United States. So any ideas into keeping the Magicsaber of Darkness from effecting anyone on our way to my house?" Kimberly asked.

Sergeant Bash had the answer "When we discovered the Magicsabers of Light and Darkness, we discovered that the Magicsaber of Darkness was wrapped up in a piece of cloth therefore when we gripped it. It didn't put its spell on us, by rewrapping it up in it's cloth we can stop it from using it's spell on people."

Jack nodded "That's right my Nutralisk Forces found the cloth and we still have it." The Nutralisk leader pulled the cloth out of it.

Kimberly carefully ignited the Magicsaber of Light and gently knelt down and picked up the Magicsaber of Darkness immediately doing so the two Magicsabers went right to work.

"Hurry, arggh! They're using magic again!" Kimberly said as Jack rushed towards her. Kimberly let the Magicsaber of Darkness drop onto the cloth immediately the blade stopped humming as Jack Latient tried to wrap it up. Jack tried to wrap it up but was still afraid of its powerful ability. Even if it wasen't humming a direct touch could still kill in one blow. Kimberly got an idea.

"Jack use Terror's legs" she suggested after a while.

Jack nodded and picked up Terror's bottom half and with the destroyed drone's leg touched the blade's ignition switch. Immediately Jack wrapped the cloth out without fear as he saw it disappear.

"Excuse me" Flower said taking the bottom half of Terror's body from Jack as he completed wrapping it up. Both the Nutralisk leader and Kimberly saw what happened next. Flower took Terror's bottom half and slammed it into the wall in her anger.

"You big bully! Ripping my throat out. Then trying to kill my best childhood friend. Looks like she taught you! Take this, this and this!"

She slammed the bottom half onto the wall of the castle until all of it's legs were broken of and his body utterly destroyed. Then she moved onto his upper form and slammed it against the wall.

"Well. I think she's became a lot braver now," a mechanical voice said.

"Terror your dead" Flower jumped away just as Destructor came into the room.

"Oh great the New Terror the Assassin!" Kent said.

"Duck Commander Flower!" the Assassin drone commanded.

Without needing any other information Commander Greendeath showed up and fired a missile filled with his radiation at Flower's head. Destructor: the last of the Assassin Drones ran towards Flower and then with his mechanical voice sounded to Magic Force and all of their allies "Run! I'll by you time."

Kimberly looked at Flower and asked as she ran to the Black Thunder along with her force, the Nutralisk Forces, and what was left of the USA army "What have you done to that Assassin Drone?"

Flower heard an explosion followed by a load groan from Destructor and by the words from Greendeath "Fool, betrayed by my own men and a trusted Commander. It wasen't meant for you I guess I should snipe her out."

Flower turned to her friends "Let's just say I had a conversation with Destructor. He was only a drone working for Terror only cause Terror controlled his army with an iron fist."

"So I guess there are good drones even in Terror's empire after all" General Goldsupervena said.

Behind them, they heard Greendeath following them. Suddenly they turned to see Destructor chasing Greendeath.

"Let her go Greendeath" Destructor warned.

"Well what's wrong with you Terror's dead plus Railbuster is still here, I'll turn you over to him" Greendeath said.

Goldsupervena couldn't stop to mind his words "Hey, Railbuster is destroyed! I defeated him leave that Assassin Drone alone!"

Kimberly turned to Goldsupervena "Gee, I thought you didn't like Assassin Drones."

"I didn't like Terror but Destructor's different," Goldsupervena said.

"Like Flower said, he's one of Terror's nice drones. I'm going to save him with my luck we can repair him" Goldsupervena said charging Greendeath.

Greendeath looked behind him to see General Goldsupervena as he shot another nuclear missile at Destructor the Assassin Drone fell almost immune to the radiation. However he was not immune to missile explosions. The now brave and heroic Assassin Drone ignored his wounds and kept charging Greendeath. Greendeath turned and fired at Goldsupervena. The Battlebot General used his Magicsaber and reflected the blast back towards Greendeath. Greendeath stumbled but into Destructor's range.

"Wait Destructor don't do this to me!" Greendeath said with naked fear in his eyes.

"Never! You're the type of scum that will kill a girl for calling you names, and besides I've never liked Terror, but I had to or else… Death. Now it's time for me to recover the bad deeds Terror had done to us. Time for you my friend to die!" with those words said the

Assassin Drone flung himself upon Greendeath and in three seconds ripped Greendeath to shreds.

Destructor turned to General Goldsupervena "Hi, you came to destroy me didn't you. Well it's the least I can do. Go ahead destroy me for taking Flower to Terror."

The Battlebot General Goldsupervena looked at Destructor "No, by destroying Greendeath you proved to me Assassin Drones can be good. I want to repay you for your kindness follow me," Goldsupervena said.

"Okay" Destructor said.

Kimberly was waiting for Goldsupervena to come near the Black Thunder.

"I see someone made a new friend," she said smiling to the Battlebot and Assassin Drone.

Destructor nodded and gave Kimberly the Magicsaber of Darkness wrapped up "He did, he spared me um here you go. You left without this."

Kimberly accepted the gift "Thank you I'll get some worker bots to repair you on our flight back to my house."

Destructor nodded "I am happy that I turned against Terror and will be much grateful to you if I could be repaired."

"Good I'll send Dr. Lightspirit out to repair you on the flight" Kimberly said.

"Since when did I become a robot doctor?" Lightspirit asked himself.

"Thanks Lady Kimberly" Destructor said.

With those words said the three friends walked into the Black Thunder.

Chapter 16
Reunion

Kimberly's mother sat around the house. Every day her daughter was away she was worried. Kent's mother and sister came by every day sharing and wondering the same ideas. The two families tried to cheer themselves up.

Kimberly's school became more and more involved with the procedure; the school had their children prey for Kimberly hoping that she and her friends Kent, and Flower were safe. Most girls however preyed for Moonshine's safe return. Many boys wanted to polish Goldsupervena again.

Suddenly on a Saturday morning they saw a mean looking black fighter jet rushing towards them. Kids were scared as Magic Tanks, Nutralisk Leaf Tanks came into view. Kimberly's mother saw the ship land. It opened its hatch and Goldsupervena rushed out. All boys rushed towards the Battlebot with polishing cloths ready.

Goldsupervena shook his head at them and held out his right hand at them "Not yet gentlemen."

Both young boys and girls stopped as an Assassin Drone came out. "Terror run!" the boys shouted.

Kimberly's mother along with Kent's mother and sister backed up a bit but grew calmer when they released the Assassin Drone didn't jump into Goldsupervena and rip him to shreds.

Destructor the last of Terror's Assassin Drones jumped down near Kimberly's mother startling her for a minute.

"I'm sorry for my leaders actions. I was powerless to help" Destructor said.

Kimberly's mother understood the Assassin Drone.

"I get it so not all Assassin Drones are evil," she said.

"Yes, you definitely got it. If I could've saved him I would've just as I saved Flower from Greendeath" Destructor said.

"Okay your asking for forgiveness aren't you?" Kent's mother asked.

"Yes, I am destroy me if you must" Destructor said.

"No need to" Kimberly's mother said looking at the Assassin Drone "But one thing bothers me is my daughter alive. Has she been killed?"

Goldsupervena sighed and Kimberly's mother grew worried "You said you'd protect her!"

Destructor and the Battlebot roared with laughter "That's a good one General Goldsupervena making her mother think she's gone!" Destructor said.

"You mean she isn't?"

Goldsupervena nodded his head "Yes madme she's alive."

With that Kimberly walked through the door of the Black Thunder.

Kimberly's mother ran out and hugged her daughter fondly "You made it Kimberly."

Destructor turned to the crowd most of the crowd still feared the Assassin Drone thinking it was Terror and backed away.

"I'm not Terror!" the Assassin Drone said waving his claws to sides trying to convince them.

Kimberly's mother looked at her daughter as everyone came out of the Black Thunder "So Kimberly did you convince yourself not to continue the war against Terror?"

"Why do you ask mom?" Kimberly asked hugging her mother fondly.

"Because your home earlier than I expected."

"We completed it! We won the war. Destructor just made the surrender plus he helped us escape by destroying Greendeath" Kimberly said.

"Destructor thank you for saving her"

"No problem lady, it was the least I could do for both sides. Then in the Black Thunder, I surrendered not wanting to be considered evil," the assassin drone said.

"He did well to, the Machine-Assassin Empire has fallen and only has about fifty units alive" Goldsupervena said.

"Heres the good part that fifty is all good drones and I knew that's not enough to continue war but to tell you the truth I hate war" the Assassin drone told the crowd.

Turning to the crowd Kimberly raised her hands for silence as the crowd cheered. When silence came, Kimberly looked in the crowd and in her best of her abilities tried to speak like the leader she was.

"Everyone! Magic Force won the war as you can see. Now we have a surprise to you! Terror tried to consume the evil powers of the Magicsaber of Darkness! It is too powerful for anyone to get his or her hands on it. So for my last good deed before Magic Force becomes peaceful, we will destroy the very evil which started the bloody war in the first place!"

Carefully and steadily Lightspirit and Kent carried the Magicsaber of Darkness in it's cloth still glowing but unaffecting them.

Goldsupervena accepted the Magicsaber of Darkness's handle. Moonshine came out quite dizzy from the flight.

"Next time Kimberly, I drive the Black Thunder," the unicorn said falling out of the Black Thunder's opened door.

"Moonshine I need help destroying this evil blade!" Goldsupervena said trying to snap the blade clean.

"Oh? Right!" Moonshine said snapping out of her status.

Professor Strike appeared and the good professor said in his best speaking voice "The time has come my friends! The time to bring peace to our country! General Goldsupervena and General Moonshine will use their powers to destroy the Magicsaber of Darkness!"

"There can only be one Magicsaber of something and that something is the Magicsaber of Light!" Kimberly said.

"That's correct!" Destructor said.

Goldsupervena held the blade by it's handle and squeezed with all his might. Moonshine gently closed her eyes and released all of her magical abilities to the fullest. With a gleaming white light and with Goldsupervena's unbearable strength destroyed the blade into millions of pieces. Goldsupervena let go of the Magicsaber of Darkness and let the pieces fall onto the ground. The crowd went wild and cheered as the pieces fell onto the ground.

"Now Lightspirit send these pieces across the galaxy for I fear that someone could make it back together. The pieces that lay here will soon be put back together" Kimberly said to Lightspirit.

The Battlebot nodded and spread his paws "Right Magic Control!" a bright blue beam came out and caught the two blades and transported the pieces everywhere over the Earth.

Kimberly's mother hugged her daughter fondly as the crowd cheered now that the Magicsaber of Darkness was destroyed and sent to a dimension. The president's limo filled with himself and the Secretary of Defense came into view. The President stepped out of the limo with his Secretary. The President and Secretary came towards Kimberly.

"Sorry that we missed the sight of the Magicsaber of Darkness being destroyed and sent" the President said.

Kimberly and her two generals looked at the President but Kimberly spoke to the United States of America's president formally "Mr. President it's okay, the war against Terror and his forces is over with a win for Magic Force, it's allies the Nutralisk and what was left of the USA army lead by Jack Latient the Nutralisk leader and Sergeant Bash the USA army leader.

The president nodded "True your too true. Listen your definitely Magic Force's leader Lady Kimberly. We the people of the USA have guaranteed that your forces are heroes," the Secretary of Defence said.

Kimberly was taken back "You mean to say that…"

"Yes, Lady Kimberly you and your forces are nominated as a powerful army. The Nutralisk are another army that is allied to you since it is a permanent alliance. Now for Destructor's cause" the President said turning to Destructor when he said Destructor's cause.

"Go ahead punish me for Terror's dreadful act!"

"I won't in fact I'd like to give you a new territory. Where you can rule" the President said.

"Oh, well were drones! We can live on the Moon" Destructor said.

"That's what I was referring to," the President said.

"Then I'll go but first, Kimberly can I be an ally to you?"

Kimberly turned to Destructor and thought of Destructor's offer before replying "Um sure but what would the other drones think?"

"Well, my people will go onto the Moon under my leadership. I won't be as hard as Terror was on them but will use the powers of my army for good. If they have a say to it then let them speak to me. I'll handle it properly," Destructor said.

"Good, then permanent alliance accepted" Kimberly said to him shaking his hand.

"Good then, maybe well see each other again someday" Destructor said leaving.

"Oh becareful, my astronauts will take you to the Moon where you can start a new life" the President said.

"Oh that'll be fine" Destructor said as he got in the car with the President and the President's Secretary of Defence.

Kimberly watched them drive off before turning to the crowd

"Today we celebrate the day of our victory! Let this day well be remembered in American History. Magic Force has been born and I will stop any threat that dares to come to Earth this I swear!"

With lots of cheering from the crowd, the victorious Magic Force along with it's allies celebrated!

Epilogue
Exact Writings in Kimberly's Diary

Dear Diary,

Two days have passed since our extreme victory over Terror's Forces. Peace is ringing in my ears. The sound of the birds singing is really soothing. Oh but that isn't what I am writing about today. Today I'm writing about my friends. General Goldsupervena has been a great friend. The Battlebot general is helping my mother preparing food, protecting me and every day I was at school, boys would always polish him daily. General Moonshine is very popular among the female students in my school every time I take her to school they always groom her mane. Flower, my dearest of all friends and I are getting popular in school. Not only do we get the credit of defeating the ultimate Terror's army but also we get out of school an hour early. Kent and I have been getting closer to each other. Just the other day he asked me to help him, and his father on a project. Of course I said yes, which I shouldn't have though, for Lightspirit was also helping them. Yeah you can bet I groaned when he started to preach about the word of the Gods. Fortunately unlike

Goldsupervena, Lightspirit was kind of dull and didn't seem to know that the groan was an insult. Then why am I saying this when I have the crazy idea of giving him the title of Magic Force's preacher? Maybe Moonshine knows she'll answer me hopefully. Jack is leading his Nutralisk far and wide helping police to catch most wanted criminals. Sniper is watching over all of us from the longest distance he can. Good for him and all the other members of Magic Force for just the other day, some man grabbed me and demeaned that I was to give him my Magicsaber of Light. I just couldn't surrender the marvelous blade Goldsupervena gave me so I kicked him. Right then when I turned around I heard a shot and when I looked at the man, he was dead with an arrow and bullet wound. I was thankful for that. Now what else is there? Oh yeah Destructor. Well Destructor has actually succeeded Terror's position and as promised kept his drones from killing any people he has changed the name of the Machine Assassin Empire to Metal Law Enforcement Democracy. I'm happy for that Drone. Sometimes I imagine that Magic Force is at war and on its side fighting on our side along with the Nutralisk Force and the USA Army. What am I thinking? I shouldn't be thinking of war! I hate it. Well before I hurt myself I am putting you down now. Sighed Kimberly leader of Magic Force.

The End.